Avluela said, 'When we stood before the globe of the world, you said you were unable to find the place where you were born on the map. Tell me now: are you what you say you are, a Changeling who wanders the world?'

He replied, 'I am not. I was born nowhere on this globe, but on a world of a star I must not name. I have lived here ten years.'

'What was your purpose in coming to Earth?' I asked. He smiled. 'I was sent to Earth in the capacity of a military observer, to prepare the way for the invasion for which you have watched so long and in which you have ceased to believe, and which will be upon you in a matter now of some hours.'

'Lies!' I bellowed. '*Lies!*'....

Also by Robert Silverberg in Sphere Books:
TO OPEN THE SKY

Nightwings
ROBERT SILVERBERG

SPHERE BOOKS LIMITED
30/32 Gray's Inn Road, London WC1X 8JL

First published in Great Britain by Sidgwick & Jackson Ltd 1972
Copyright © Galaxy Publishing Corporation 1968, 1969
First Sphere Books edition 1974
Reprinted 1978, 1983

TRADE
MARK

Set in Linotype Plantin

Printed in Great Britain by
Hazell Watson & Viney Ltd
Aylesbury, Bucks

For Harlan,
to remind him of open windows,
the currents of the Delaware River,
quarters with two heads,
and other pitfalls.

PART I

NIGHTWINGS

1

ROUM is a city built on seven hills. They say it was a capital of man in one of the earlier cycles. I did not know of that, for my guild was Watching, not Remembering; but yet as I had my first glimpse of Roum, coming upon it from the south at twilight, I could see that in former days it must have been of great significance. Even now it was a mighty city of many thousands of souls.

Its bony towers stood out sharply against the dusk. Lights glimmered appealingly. On my left hand the sky was ablaze with splendor as the sun relinquished possession; streaming bands of azure and violet and crimson folded and writhed about one another in the nightly dance that brings the darkness. To my right, blackness had already come. I attempted to find the seven hills, and failed, and still I knew that this was that Roum of majesty toward which all roads are bent, and I felt awe and deep respect for the works of our bygone fathers.

We rested by the long straight road, looking up at Roum. I said, 'It is a goodly city. We will find employment there.'

Beside me, Avluela fluttered her lacy wings. 'And food?' she asked in her high, fluty voice. 'And shelter? And wine?'

'Those too,' I said. 'All of those.'

'How long have we been walking, Watcher?' she asked.

'Two days. Three nights.'

'If I had been flying, it would have been more swift.'

'For you,' I said. 'You would have left us far behind and never seen us again. Is that your desire?'

She came close to me and rubbed the rough fabric of my sleeve, and then she pressed herself at me the way a flirting cat might do. Her wings unfolded into two broad sheets of gossamer through which I could still see the sunset and

7

the evening lights, blurred, distorted, magical. I sensed the fragrance of her midnight hair. I put my arms to her and embraced her slender, boyish body.

She said, 'You know it is my desire to remain with you always, Watcher. Always!'

'Yes, Avluela.'

'Will we be happy in Roum?'

'We will be happy,' I said, and released her.

'Shall we go into Roum now?'

'I think we should wait for Gormon,' I said, shaking my head. 'He'll be back soon from his explorations.' I did not want to tell her of my weariness. She was only a child, seventeen summers old; what did she know of weariness or of age? And I was old. Not as old as Roum, but old enough.

'While we wait,' she said, 'may I fly?'

'Fly, yes.'

I squatted beside our cart and warmed my hands at the throbbing generator while Avluela prepared to fly. First she removed her garments, for her wings have little strength and she cannot lift such extra baggage. Lithely, deftly, she peeled the glassy bubbles from her tiny feet and wriggled free of her crimson jacket and of her soft furry leggings. The vanishing light in the west sparkled over her slim form. Like all Fliers, she carried no surplus body tissue: her breasts were mere bumps, her buttocks flat, her thighs so spindly that there was a span of inches between them when she stood. Could she have weighed more than a quintal? I doubt it. Looking at her, I felt, as always, gross and earthbound, a thing of loathsome flesh, and yet I am not a heavy man.

By the roadside she genuflected knuckles to the ground, head bowed to knees, as she said whatever ritual it is that the Fliers say. Her back was to me. Her delicate wings fluttered, filled with life, rose about her like a cloak whipped up by the breeze. I could not comprehend how such wings could possibly life even so slight a form as Avluela's. They were not hawk-like but butterfly-wings, veined and transparent, marked here and there with blotches of pigment, ebony and turquoise and scarlet. A sturdy ligament joined them to the two flat pads of muscle beneath her sharp shoulderblades; but what she did not have was the massive

8

breastbone of a flying creature, the bands of corded muscle needed for flight. Oh, I know that Fliers use more than muscle to get aloft, that there are mystical disciplines in their mystery. Even so, I, who was of the Watchers, remained skeptical of the more fantastic guilds.

Avluela finished her words. She rose; she caught the breeze with her wings; she ascended several feet. There she remained, suspended between earth and sky, while her wings beat frantically. It was not yet night, and Avluela's wings were merely nightwings. By day she could not fly, for the terrible pressure of the solar wind would hurl her to the ground. Now, midway between dusk and dark, it was still not the best time for her to go up. I saw her thrust toward the east by the remnant of light in the sky. Her arms as well as her wings thrashed; her small pointed face was grim with concentration; on her thin lips were the words of her guild. She doubled her body and shot it out, head going one way, rump the other; and abruptly she hovered horizontally, looking groundward, her wings thrashing against the air. *Up, Avluela! Up!*

Up it was, as by will alone she conquered the vestige of light that still glowed.

With pleasure I surveyed her naked form against the darkness. I could see her clearly, for a Watcher's eyes are keen. She was five times her own height in the air, now, and her wings spread to their full expanse, so that the towers of Roum were in partial eclipse for me. She waved. I threw her a kiss and offered words of love. Watchers do not marry, nor do they engender children, but yet Avluela was as a daughter to me, and I took pride in her flight. We had travelled together a year, now, since we had first met in Agupt, and it was as though I had known her all my life. From her I drew a renewal of strength. I do not know what it was she drew from me: security, knowledge, a continuity with the days before her birth. I hoped only that she loved me as I loved her.

Now she was far aloft. She wheeled, soared, dived, pirouetted, danced. Her long black hair streamed from her scalp. Her body seemed only an incidental appendage to those two great wings which glistened and throbbed and gleamed in the night. Up she rose, glorying in her freedom from gravity, making me feel all the more leaden-footed;

9

and like some slender rocket she shot abruptly away in the direction of Roum. I saw the soles of her feet, the tips of her wings; then I saw her no more.

I sighed. I thrust my hands into the pits of my arms to keep them warm. How is it that I felt a winter chill while the girl Avluela could soar joyously bare through the sky?

It was the twelfth of the twenty hours, and time once again for me to do the Watching. I went to the cart, opened my cases, prepared the instruments. Some of the dial covers were yellowed and faded; the indicator needles had lost their luminous coating; sea stains defaced the instrument housings, a relic of the time that pirates had assailed me in Earth Ocean. The worn and cracked levers and nodes responded easily to my touch as I entered the preliminaries. First one prays for a pure and perceptive mind; then one creates the affinity with one's instruments; then one does the actual Watching, searching the starry heavens for the enemies of man. Such was my skill and my craft. I grasped handles and knobs, thrust things from my mind, prepared myself to become an extension of my cabinet of devices.

I was only just past my threshold and into the first phase of Watchfulness when a deep and resonant voice behind me said, 'Well, Watcher, how goes it?'

I sagged against the cart. There is a physical pain in being wrenched so unexpectedly from one's work. For a moment I felt claws clutching at my heart. My face grew hot; my eyes would not focus; the saliva drained from my throat. As soon as I could, I took the proper protective measures to ease the metabolic drain, and severed myself from my instruments. Hiding my trembling as much as possible, I turned round.

Gormon, the other member of our little band, had appeared and stood jauntily beside me. He was grinning, amused at my distress, but I could not feel angry with him. One does not show anger at a guildless person no matter what the provocation.

Tightly, with effort, I said, 'Did you spend your time rewardingly?'

'Very. Where's Avluela?'

I pointed heavenward. Gormon nodded.

'What have you found?' I asked.

'That this city is definitely Roum.'

10

'There never was doubt of that.'

'For me there was. But now I have proof.'

'Yes?'

'In the overpocket. Look!'

From his tunic he drew his overpocket, set it on the pavement beside me, and expanded it so that he could insert his hands into its mouth. Grunting a little, he began to pull something heavy from the pouch – something of white stone – a long marble column, I now saw, fluted, pocked with age.

'From a temple of Imperial Roum!' Gormon exulted.

'You shouldn't have taken that.'

'Wait!' he cried, and reached into the overpocket once more. He took from it a handful of circular metal plaques and scattered them jingling at my feet. 'Coins! Money! Look at them, Watcher! The faces of the Caesars!'

'Of whom?'

'The ancient rulers. Don't you know your history of past cycles?'

I peered at him curiously. 'You claim to have no guild, Gormon. Could it be you are a Rememberer and are concealing it from me?'

'Look at my face, Watcher. Could I belong to any guild? Would a Changeling be taken?'

'True enough,' I said, eying the golden hue of him, the thick waxen skin, the red-pupiled eyes, the jagged mouth. Gormon had been weaned on teratogenetic drugs; he was a monster, handsome in his way, but a monster nevertheless, a Changeling, outside the laws and customs of man as they are practised in the Third Cycle of civilization. And there is no guild of Changelings.

'There's more,' Gormon said. The overpocket was infinitely capacious, the contents of a world, if need be, could be stuffed into its shriveled gray maw, and still it would be no longer than a man's hand. Gormon took from it bits of machinery, reading spools, an angular thing of brown metal that might have been an ancient tool, three squares of shining glass, five slips of paper – *paper!* – and a host of other relics of antiquity. 'See?' he said. 'A fruitful stroll, Watcher! And not just random booty. Everything recorded, everything labeled, stratum, estimated age, position when *in situ*. Here we have many thousands of years of Roum.'

'Should you have taken these things?' I asked doubtfully.

'Why not? Who is to miss them? Who of this cycle cares for the past?'

'The Rememberers.'

'They don't need solid objects to help them do their work.'

'Why do you want these things, though?'

'The past interests me, Watcher. In my guildless way I have my scholarly pursuits. Is that wrong? May not even a monstrosity seek knowledge?'

'Certainly, certainly. Seek what you wish. Fulfill yourself in your own way. This is Roum. At dawn we enter. I hope to find employment here.'

'You may have difficulties.'

'How so?'

'There are many Watchers already in Roum, no doubt. There will be little need for your services.'

'I'll seek the favour of the Prince of Roum,' I said.

'The Prince of Roum is a hard and cold and cruel man.'

'You know of him?'

Gormon shrugged. 'Somewhat.' He bagan to stuff his artifacts back in the overpocket. 'Take your chances with him, Watcher. What other choice do you have?'

'None,' I said, and Gormon laughed, and I did not.

He busied himself with his ransacked loot of the past. I found myself deeply depressed by his words. He seemed so sure of himself in an uncertain world, this guildless one, this mutated monster, this man of inhuman look; how could he be so cool, so casual? He lived without concern for calamity and mocked those who admitted to fear. Gormon had been traveling with us for nine days, now, since we had met him in the ancient city beneath the volcano to the south by the edge of the sea. I had not suggested that he join us; he had invited himself along, and at Avluela's bidding I accepted. The roads are dark and cold at this time of year, and dangerous beasts of many species abound, and an old man journeying with a girl might well consider taking with him a brawny one like Gormon. Yet there times I wished he had not come with us, and this was one.

Slowly I walked back to my equipment.

Gormon said, as though first realizing it, 'Did I interrupt you at your Watching?'

12

I said mildly, 'You did.'

'Sorry. Go and start again. I'll leave you in peace.' And he gave me his dazzling lopsided smile, so full of charm that it took the curse off the easy arrogance of his words.

I touched the knobs, made contact with the nodes, monitored the dials. But I did not enter Watchfulness, for I remained aware of Gormon's presence and fearful that he would break into my concentration once again at a painful moment, despite his promise. At length I looked away from the apparatus. Gormon stood at the far side of the road, craning his neck for some sight of Avluela. The moment I turned to him he became aware of me.

'Something wrong, Watcher?'

'No. The moment's not propitious for my work. I'll wait.'

'Tell me,' he said. 'When Earth's enemies really do come from the stars, will your machines let you know it?'

'I trust they will.'

'And then?'

'Then?'

'Then I notify the Defenders.'

'After which your life's work is over?'

'Perhaps,' I said.

'Why a whole guild of you, though? Why not one master center where the Watch is kept? Why a bunch of itinerant Watchers drifting from place to place?'

'The more vectors of detection,' I said, 'the greater the chance of early awareness of the invasion.'

'Then an individual Watcher might well turn his machines on and not see anything, with an invader already here.'

'It could happen. And so we practice redundancy.'

'You carry it to an extreme, I sometimes think.' Gormon laughed. 'Do you actually believe an invasion is coming?'

'I do,' I said stiffly. 'Else my life was a waste.'

'And why should the star people want Earth? What do we have besides the remnants of old empires? What would they do with miserable Roum? With Perris? With Jorslem? Rotting cities! Idiot princes! Come, Watcher, admit it: the invasion's a myth, and you go through meaningless motions four times a day. Eh?'

'It is my craft and my science to Watch. It is yours to jeer. Each of us to our speciality, Gormon.'

13

'Forgive me,' he said with mock humility. 'Go, then, and Watch.'

'I shall.'

Angrily I turned back to my cabinet of instruments, determined now to ignore any interruption, no matter how brutal. The stars were out; I gazed at the glowing constellations, and automatically my mind registered the many worlds. Let us Watch, I thought. Let us keep our vigil despite the mockers.

I entered full Watchfulness.

I clung to the grips and permitted the surge of power to rush through me. I cast my mind to the heavens and searched for hostile entities. What ecstasy! What incredible splendor! I who had never left this small planet roved the black spaces of the void, glided from star to burning star, saw the planets spinning like tops. Faces stared back at me as I journeyed, some without eyes, some with many eyes, all the complexity of the many-peopled galaxy accessible to me. I spied out possible concentrations of inimicable force. I inspected drilling grounds and military encampments. I sought four times daily for all my adult life, for the invaders who had been promised us, the conquerors who at the end of days were destined to seize our tattered world.

I found nothing, and when I came up from my trance, sweaty and drained, I saw Avluela descending.

Feather-light she landed. Gormon called to her, and she ran, bare, her little breasts quivering, and he enfolded her smallness in his powerful arms, and they embraced, not passionately but joyously. When he released her she turned to me.

'Roum,' she gasped. '*Roum!*'

'You saw it?'

'Everything! Thousands of people! Lights! Boulevards! A market! Broken buildings many cycles old! Oh, Watcher, how wonderful Roum is!'

'Your flight was a good one, then,' I said.

'A miracle!'

'Tomorrow we go to dwell in Roum.'

'No, Watcher, tonight, tonight!' She was girlishly eager, her face bright with excitement. 'It's just a short journey more! Look, it's just over there!'

14

'We should rest first,' I said. 'We do not want to arrive weary in Roum.'

'We can rest when we get there,' Avluela answered. 'Come! Pack everything! You've done your Watching, haven't you?'

'Yes. Yes.'

'Then let's go. To Roum! To Roum!'

I looked in appeal at Gormon. Night had come; it was time to make camp, to have our few hours of sleep.

For once Gormon sided with me. He said to Avluela. 'The Watcher's right. We can all use some rest. We'll go on into Roum at Dawn.'

Avluela pouted. She looked more like a child than ever. Her wings drooped, her underdeveloped body slumped. Petulantly she closed her wings until they were mere fist-sized humps on her back, and picked up the garments she had scattered on the road. She dressed while we made camp. I distributed food tablets; we entered our receptacles; I fell into troubled sleep and dreamed of Avluela limned against the crumbling moon, and Gormon flying beside her. Two hours before dawn I arose and performed my first watch of the new day, while they still slept. Then I aroused them, and we went onward toward the fabled imperial city, onward toward Roum.

2

THE morning's light was bright and harsh, as though this were some young world newly created. The road was all but empty; people do not travel much in these latter days unless, like me, they are wanderers by habit and profession. Occasionally we stepped aside to let a chariot of some member of the guild of Masters go by, drawn by a dozen expressionless neuters harnessed in series. Four such vehicles went by in the first two hours of the day, each shuttered and sealed to hide the Master's proud features from the gaze of such common folk as we. Several rollerwagons laden with produce passed us, and a number of floaters soared overhead. Generally we had the road to ourselves, however.

The environs of Roum showed vestiges of antiquity: isolated columns, the fragments of an aqueduct transporting nothing from nowhere to nowhere, the portals of a vanished temple. That was the oldest Roum we saw, but there were accretions of the later Roums of subsequent cycles: the huts of peasants, the domes of power drains, the hulls of dwelling-towers. Infrequently we met with the burned-out shell of some ancient airship. Gormon examined everything, taking samples from time to time. Avluela looked, wide-eyed, saying nothing. We walked on, until the walls of the city loomed before us.

They were of a blue glossy stone, neatly joined, rising to a height of perhaps eight men. Our road pierced the wall through a corbeled arch; the gate stood open. As we approached the gate a figure came toward us; he was hooded, masked, a man of extraordinary height wearing the somber garb of the guild of Pilgrims. One does not approach such a person oneself, but one heeds him if he beckons. The Pilgrim beckoned.

Through his speaking grille he said, 'Where from?'

'The south. I lived in Agupt awhile, then crossed Land Bridge to Talya,' I replied.

'Where bound?'

'Roum, awhile.'

'How goes the Watch?'

'As customary.'

'You have a place to stay in Roum?' the Pilgrim asked. I shook my head. 'We trust to the kindness of the Will.'

'The Will is not always kind,' said the Pilgrim absently. 'Nor is there much need of Watchers in Roum. Why do you travel with a Flier?'

'For company's sake. And because she is young and needs protection.'

'Who is the other one?'

'He is guildless, a Changeling.'

'So I can see. But why is he with you?'

'He is strong and I am old, and so we travel together. Where are you bound, Pilgrim?'

'Jorslem. Is there another destination for my guild?'

I conceded the point with a shrug.

The Pilgrim said, 'Why do you not come to Jorslem with me?'

'My road lies north now. Jorslem is in the south, close by Agrup.'

'You have been to Agrup and not to Jorslem?' he said, puzzled.

'Yes. The time was not ready for me to see Jorslem.'

'Come now. We will walk together on the road, Watcher, and we will talk of the old times and of the times to come, and I will assist you in your Watching, and you will assist me in my communions with the Will. Is it agreed?'

It was a temptation. Before my eyes flashed the image of Jorslem the Golden, its holy buildings and shrines, its places of renewal where the old are made young, its spires, its tabernacles. Even though I am a man set in his ways, I was willing at the moment to abandon Roum and go with the Pilgrim to Jorslem.

I said, 'And my companions—'

'Leave them. It is forbidden for me to travel with the guildless, and I do not wish to travel with a female. You and I, Watcher, will go to Jorslem together.'

Avluela, who had been standing to one side frowning through all this colloquy, shot me a look of sudden terror.

'I will not abandon them,' I said.

'Then I go to Jorslem alone,' said the Pilgrim. Out of his

17

robe stretched a bony hand, the fingers long and white and steady. I touched my fingers reverently to the tips of his, and the Pilgrim said, 'Let the Will give you mercy, friend Watcher. And when you reach Jorslem, search for me.'

He moved on down the road without further conversation.

Gormon said to me, 'You would have gone with him, wouldn't you?'

'I considered it.'

'What could you find in Jorslem that isn't here? That's a holy city and so is this. Here you can rest awhile. You're in no shape for more walking now.'

'You may be right,' I conceded, and with the last of my energy I strode toward the gate of Roum.

Watchful eyes scanned us from slots in the wall. When we were at midpoint in the gate, a fat, pockmarked Sentinel with sagging jowls halted us and asked our business in Roum. I stated my guild and purpose, and he gave a snort of disgust.

'Go elsewhere, Watcher! We need only useful men here.'

'Watching has its uses,' I said mildly.

'No doubt. No doubt.' He squinted at Avluela. 'Who's this? Watchers are celibates, no?'

'She is nothing more than a traveling companion.'

The Sentinel guffawed coarsely. 'It's a route you travel often, I wager! Not that there's much to her. What is she, thirteen, fourteen? Come here, child. Let me check you for contraband.' He ran his hands quickly over her, scowling as he felt her breasts, then raising an eyebrow as he encountered the mounds of her wings below her shoulders. 'What's this? What's this? More in back than in front! A Flier, are you? Very dirty business, Fliers consorting with foul old Watchers.' He chuckled and put his hand on Avluela's body in a way that sent Gormon starting forward in fury, murder in his fire-circled eyes. I caught him in time and grasped his wrist with all my strength, holding him back lest he ruin the three of us by an attack on the Sentinel. He tugged at me, nearly pulling me over; then he grew calm and subsided, icily watching as the fat one finished checking Avluela for 'contraband.'

At length the Sentinel turned in distaste to Gormon and said, 'What kind of thing are you?'

'Guildless, your mercy,' Gormon said in sharp tones. 'The

18

humble and worthless product of teratogenesis, and yet nevertheless a free man who desires entry to Roum.'

'Do we need more monsters here?'

'I eat little and work hard.'

'You'd work harder still if you were neutered,' said the Sentinel.

Gormon glowered. I said, 'May we have entry?'

'A moment.' The Sentinel donned his thinking cap and narrowed his eyes as he transmitted a message to the memory tanks. His face tensed with the effort; then it went slack, and moments later came the reply. We could not hear the transaction at all; but from his disappointed look, it appeared evident that no reason had been found to refuse us admission to Roum.

'Go on in,' he said. 'The three of you. Quickly!'

We passed beyond the gate.

Gormon said, 'I could have split him open with a blow.'

'And be neutered by nightfall. A little patience, and we've come into Roum.'

'The way he handled her——!'

'You have a very possessive attitude toward Avluela,' I said. 'Remember that she's a Flier, and not sexually available to the guildless.'

Gormon ignored my thrust. 'She arouses me no more than you do, Watcher. But it pains me to see her treated that way. I would have killed him if you hadn't held me back.'

Avluela said, 'Where shall we stay, now that we're in Roum?'

'First let me find the headquarters of my guild,' I said. 'I'll register at the Watchers' Inn. After that, perhaps we'll hunt up the Fliers' Lodge for a meal.'

'And then,' said Gormon drily, 'we'll go to the Guildless Gutter and beg for coppers.'

'I pity you because you are a Changeling,' I told him, 'but I find it ungraceful of you to pity yourself. Come.'

We walked up a cobbled, winding street away from the gate and into Roum itself. We were in the outer ring of the city, a residential section of low, squat houses topped by the unwielding bulk of defense installations. Within lay the shining towers we had seen from the fields the night before; the remnant of ancient Roum carefully preserved across ten thousand years or more; the market, the factory zone, the communications hump, the temples of the Will, the memory tanks, the sleepers' refuges, the outworlders' brothels, the government buildings, the headquarters of the various guilds.

At the corner, beside a Second Cycle building with walls of rubbery texture, I found a public thinking cap and slipped it on my forehead. At once my thoughts raced down the conduit until they came to the interface that gave them access to one of the storage brains of a memory tank. I pierced the interface and saw the wrinkled brain itself, a pale gray against the deep green of its housing. A Rememberer once told me that, in cycles past, men built machines to do their thinking for them, although these machines were hellishly expensive and required vast amounts of space and drank power gluttonously. That was not the worst of our forefathers' follies; but why build artificial brains when death each day liberates scores of splendid natural ones to hook into the memory tanks? Was it that they lacked the knowledge to use them? I find that hard to believe.

I gave the brain my guild identification and asked the co-ordinates of our inn. Instantly I received them, and we set out, Avluela on one side of me, Gormon on the other, myself wheeling as always, the cart in which my instruments resided.

The city was crowded. I had not seen such throngs in sleepy, heat-fevered Agupt, nor at any other point on my northward journey. The streets were full of Pilgrims, secretive and masked. Jostling through them went busy Rememberers and glum Merchants and now and then the litter of a Master. Avluela saw a number of Fliers, but was barred by the tenets of her guild from greeting them until she had undergone her ritual purification. I regret to say that I spied many Watchers, all of whom looked upon me disdainfully and without welcome. I noted a good many Defenders and ample representation of such lesser guilds as Vendors, Servitors, Manufactories, Scribes, Communicants, and Transporters. Naturally, a host of neuters went silently about their humble business, and numerous outworlders of all descriptions flocked the streets, most of them probably tourists, some here to do what business could be done with the sullen, poverty-blighted people of Earth. I noticed many

20

Changelings limping furtively through the crowd, not one of them as proud of bearing as Gormon beside me. He was unique among his kind; the others, dappled and piebald and asymmetrical, limbless or overlimbed, deformed in a thousand imaginative and artistic ways, were slinkers, squinters, shufflers, hissers, creepers; they were cutpurses, brain-drainers, organ-peddlers, repentance-mongers, gleam-buyers, but none held himself upright as though he thought he were a man.

The guidance of the brain was exact, and in less than an hour of walking we arrived at the Watchers' Inn. I left Gormon and Avluela outside and wheeled my cart within.

Perhaps a dozen members of my guild lounged in the main hall. I gave them the customary sign, and they returned it languidly. Were these the guardians on whom Earth's safety depended? Simpletons and weaklings!

'Where may I register?' I asked.

'New? Where from?'

'Agupt was my last place of registry.'

'Should have stayed there. No need of Watchers here.'

'Where may I register?' I asked again.

A foppish youngster indicated a screen in the rear of the great room. I went to it, pressed my fingertips against it, was interrogated, and gave my name, which a Watcher must utter only to another Watcher and only within the precincts of an inn. A panel shot open, and a puffy-eyed man who wore the Watcher emblem on his right cheek and not on the left, signifying his high rank in the guild, spoke my name and said, 'You should have known better than to come to Roum. We're over our quota.'

'I claim lodging and employment nonetheless.'

' A man with your sense of humor should have been born into the guild of Clowns,' he said.

'I see no joke.'

'Under laws promulgated by our guild in the most recent session, an inn is under no obligation to take new lodgers once it has reached its assigned capacity. We are at our assigned capacity. Farewell, my friend.'

I was aghast. 'I know of no such regulation! This is incredible! For a guild to turn away a member from its own inn – when he arrives footsore and numb! A man of my age, having crossed Land Bridge out of Agupt, here as a

21

stranger and hungry in Roum—'

'Why did you not check with us first?'

'I had no idea it would be necessary.'

'The new regulations—'

'May the Will shrivel the new regulations!' I shouted. 'I demand lodging! To turn away one who has Watched since before you were born—'

'Easy, brother, easy.'

'Surely you have some corner where I can sleep – some crumbs to let me eat—'

Even as my tone had changed from bluster to supplication, his expression softened from indifference to mere disdain. 'We have no room. We have no food. These are hard times for our guild, you know. There is talk that we will be disbanded altogether, as a useless luxury, a drain upon the Will's resources. We are very limited in our abilities. Because Roum has a surplus of Watchers, we are all on short rations as it is, and if we admit you our rations will be all the shorter.'

'But where will I go? What shall I do?'

'I advise you,' he said blandly, 'to throw yourself upon the mercy of the Prince of Roum.'

3

OUTSIDE, I told that to Gormon, and he doubled with laughter, guffawing so furiously that the striations on his lean cheeks blazed like bloody stripes. 'The mercy of the Prince of Roum!' he repeated. 'The mercy – of the Prince of Roum—'

'It is customary for the unfortunate to seek the aid of the local ruler,' I said coldly.

'The Prince of Roum knows no mercy,' Gormon told me. 'The Prince of Roum will feed you your own limbs to ease your hunger!'

'Perhaps,' Avluela put in, 'we should try to find the Fliers' Lodge. They'll feed us there.'

'Not Gormon,' I observed. 'We have obligations to one another.'

'We could bring food out to him,' she said.

'I prefer to visit the court first,' I insisted. 'Let us make sure of our status. Afterwards we can improvise living arrangements, if we must.'

She yielded, and we made our way to the palace of the Prince of Roum, a massive building fronted by a colossal column-ringed plaza, on the far side of the river that splits the city. In the plaza we were accosted by mendicants of many sorts, some not even Earthborn; something with ropy tendrils and a corrugated, noseless face thrust itself at me and jabbered for alms until Gormon pushed it away, and moments later a second creature, equally strange, its skin pocked with luminescent craters and its limbs studded with eyes, embraced my knees and pleaded in the name of the Will for my mercy. 'I am only a poor Watcher,' I said, indicating my cart, 'and am here to gain mercy myself.' But the being persisted, sobbing out its misfortunes in a blurred, feathery voice, and in the end, to Gormon's immense disgust, I dropped a few food tablets into the shelf-like pouch on its chest. Then we muscled on toward the doors of the palace. At the portico a more horrid sight presented itself: a maimed Flier, fragile limbs bent and twisted, one wing half-unfolded and severely cropped, the other missing altogether. The Flier rushed upon Avluela, called her by a name not hers, moistened her leggings with tears so copious that the fur of them matted and stained. 'Sponsor me to the lodge,' he appealed. 'They have turned me away because I am crippled, but if you sponsor me—' Avlueva explained that she could do nothing, that she was a stranger to this lodge. The broken Flier would not release her, and Gormon with great delicacy lifted him like the bundle of dry bones that he was and set him aside. We stepped up onto the portico and at once were confronted by a trio of soft-faced neuters, who asked our business and admitted us quickly to the next line of barrier, which was manned by a pair of wizened Indexers. Speaking in unison, they queried us.

'We seek audience,' I said. 'A matter of mercy.'

'The day of audience is four days hence,' said the Indexer on the right. 'We will enter your request on the rolls.'

'We have no place to sleep!' Avluela burst out. 'We are hungry! We—'

I hushed her. Gormon, meanwhile, was groping in the mouth of his overpocket. Bright things glimmered in his hand; pieces of gold, the eternal metal, stamped with hawk-nosed, bearded faces. He had found them grubbing in the ruins. He tossed one coin to the Indexer who had refused us. The man snapped it from the air, rubbed his thumb roughly across its shining obverse, and dropped it instantly into a fold of his garment. The second Indexer waited expectantly. Smiling, Gormon gave him his coin.

'Perhaps,' I said, 'we can arrange for a special audience within.'

'Perhaps you can,' said one of the Indexers. 'Go through.'

And so we passed into the nave of the palace itself and stood in the great, echoing space, looking down the central aisle toward the shielded throne-chamber at the apse. There were more beggars in here – licensed ones holding hereditary concessions – and also throngs of Pilgrims, Communicants, Rememberers, Musicians, Scribes, and Indexers. I heard muttered prayers; I smelled the scent of spicy incense; I felt the vibration of subterranean gongs. In cycles past, this building had been a shrine of one of the old religions – the Christers, Gormon told me, making me suspect once more that he was a Rememberer masquerading as a Changeling –

and it still maintained something of its holy character even though it served as Roum's seat of secular government. But how were we to get to see the Prince? To my left I saw a small ornate chapel which a line of prosperous–looking Merchants and Landholders was slowly entering. Peering past them, I noted three skulls mounted on an interrogation fixture – a memory-tank input – and beside them, a burly Scribe. Telling Gormon and Avluela to wait for me in the aisle, I joined the line.

It moved infrequently, and nearly an hour passed before I reached the interrogation fixture. The skulls glared sightlessly at me; within their sealed crania, nutrient fluids bubbled and gurgled, caring for the dead, yet still functional, brains whose billion billion synaptic units now served as incomparable mnemonic devices. The Scribe seemed aghast to find a Watcher in this line, but before he could challenge me I blurted, 'I come as a stranger to claim the Prince's mercy. I and my companions are without lodging. My own guild has turned me away. What shall I do? How may I gain an audience?'

'Come back in four days.'

'I've slept on the road for more days than that. Now I must rest more easily.'

'A public inn—'

'But I am guilded!' I protested. 'The public inns would not admit me while my guild maintains an inn here, and my guild refuses me because of some new regulation, and – you see my predicament?'

In a wearied voice the Scribe said, 'You may have application for a special audience. It will be denied, but you may apply.'

'Where?'

'Here. State your purpose.'

I identified myself to the skulls by my public designation, listed the names and status of my two companions, and explained my case. All this was absorbed and transmitted to the ranks of brains mounted somewhere in the depths of the city, and when I was done the Scribe said, 'If the application is approved, you will be notified.'

'Meanwhile where shall I stay?'

'Close to the palace, I would suggest.'

I understood. I could join that legion of unfortunates

packing the plaza. How many of them had requested some special favor of the Prince and were still there, months or years later, waiting to be summoned to the Presence? Sleeping on stone, begging for crusts, living in foolish hope!

But I had exhausted my avenues. I returned to Gormon and Avluela, told them of the situation, and suggested that we now attempt to hunt whatever accommodations we could. Gormon, guildless, was welcome at any of the squalid public inns maintained for his kind; Avluela could probably find residence at her own guild's lodge; only I would have to sleep in the streets – and not for the first time. But I hoped that we would not have to separate. I had come to think of us as a family, strange thought though that was for a Watcher.

As we moved toward the exit, my timepiece told me softly that the hour of Watching had come round again. It was my obligation and my privilege to tend to my Watching wherever I might be, regardless of the circumstances, whenever my hour came round; and so I halted, opened the cart, activated the equipment. Gormon and Avluela stood beside me. I saw smirks and open mockery on the faces of those who passed in and out of the palace; Watching was not held in very high repute, for we had Watched so long, and the promised enemy had never come. Yet one has one's duties, comic though they may seem to others. What is a hollow ritual to some is a life's work to others. Doggedly I forced myself into a state of Watchfulness. The world melted away from me, and I plunged into the heavens. The familiar joy engulfed me; and I searched the familiar places, and some that were not so familiar, my amplified mind leaping through the galaxies in wild swoops. Was an armada massing? Were troops drilling for the conquest of Earth? Four times a day I Watched, and the other members of my guild did the same, each at slightly different hours, so that no moment went by without some vigilant mind on guard. I do not believe that that was a foolish calling.

When I came up from my trance, a brazen voice was crying, '—for the Prince of Roum! Make way for the Prince of Roum!'

I blinked and caught my breath and fought to shake off the last strands of my concentration. A gilded palanquin

26

borne by a phalanx of neuters had emerged from the rear of the palace and was proceeding down the nave toward me. Four men in the elegant costumes and brilliant masks of the guild of Masters flanked the litter, and it was preceded by a trio of Changelings, squat and broad, whose throats were so modified to imitate the sounding-boxes of bullfrogs; they emitted a trumpetlike boom of majestic sound as they advanced. It struck me as most strange that a prince would admit Changelings to his service, even ones as gifted as these.

My cart was blocking the progress of this magnificent procession, and hastily I struggled to close it and move it aside before the parade swept down upon me. Age and fear made my fingers tremble, and I could not make the sealings properly; while I fumbled in increasing clumsiness, the strutting Changelings drew so close that the blare of their throats was deafening, and Gormon attempted to aid me, forcing me to hiss at him that it is forbidden for anyone not of my guild to touch the equipment. I pushed him away; and an instant later a vanguard of neuters descended on me and prepared to scourge me from the spot with sparkling whips. 'In the Will's name,' I cried, 'I am a Watcher.'

And in antiphonal response came the deep, calm, enormous reply, 'Let him be. He is a Watcher.'

All motion ceased. The Prince of Roum had spoken.

The neuters drew back. The Changelings halted their music. The bearers of the Planquin eased it to the floor. All those in the nave of the palace had pulled back, save only Gormon and Avluela and myself. The shimmering chain-curtains of the palanquin parted. Two of the Masters hurried forward and thrust their hands through the sonic barrier within, offering aid to their monarch. The barrier died away with a whimpering buzz.

The Prince of Roum appeared.

He was so young! He was nothing more than a boy, his hair full and dark, his face unlined. But he had been born to rule, and for all his youth he was as commanding as anyone I had ever seen. His lips were thin and tightly compressed; his aquiline nose was sharp and aggressive; his eyes, deep and cold, were infinite pools. He wore the jeweled garments of the guild of Dominators, but incised

27

on his cheek was the double-barred cross of the Defenders, and around his neck he carried the dark shawl of the Rememberers. A Dominator may enrol in as many guilds as he pleases, and it would be a strange thing for a Dominator not also to be a Defender; but it startled me to find this prince a Rememberer as well. That is not normally a guild for the fierce.

He looked at me with little interest and said, 'You choose an odd place to do your Watching, old man.'

'The hour chose the place, sire,' I replied. 'I was here, and my duty compelled me. I had no way of knowing that you were about to come forth.'

'Your Watching found no enemies?'

'None, sire.'

I was about to press my luck, to take advantage of the unexpected appearance of the Prince to beg for his aid; but his interest in me died like a guttering candle as I stood there, and I did not dare call to him when his head had turned. He eyed Gormon a long moment, frowning and tugging at his chin. Then his gaze fell on Avluela. His eyes brightened. His jaw muscles flickered. His delicate nostrils widened. 'Come up here, little Flier,' he said, beckoning. 'Are you this Watcher's friend?'

She nodded, terrified.

The Prince held out a hand to her and grasped; she floated up onto the palanquin, and with a grin so evil it seemed a parody of wickedness, the young Dominator drew her through the curtain. Instantly a pair of Masters restored the sonic barrier, but the procession did not move on. I stood mute. Gormon beside me was frozen, his powerful body rigid as a rod. I wheeled my cart to a less conspicuous place. Long moments passed. The courtiers remained silent, discreetly looking away from the palanquin.

At length the curtain parted once more. Avluela came stumbling out, her face pale, her eyes blinking rapidly. She seemed dazed. Streaks of sweat gleamed on her cheeks. She nearly fell, and a neuter caught her and swung her down to floor level. Beneath her jacket her wings were partly erect, giving her a hunchbacked look and telling me that she was in great emotional distress. In ragged sliding steps she came to us, quivering, wordless; she darted a

28

glance at me and flung herself against Gormon's broad chest.

The bearers lifted the palanquin. The Prince of Roum went out from his palace.

When he was gone, Avluela stammered hoarsely, 'The Prince has granted us lodging in the royal hostelry!'

4

THE hostelkeepers, of course, would not believe us.

Guests of the Prince were housed in the royal hostelry, which was to the rear of the palace in a small garden of frostflowers and blossoming ferns. The usual inhabitants of such a hostelry were Masters and an occasional Dominator; sometimes a particularly important Rememberer on an errand of research would win a niche there, or some highly placed Defender visiting for purposes of strategic planning. To house a Flier in a royal hostelry was distinctly odd; to admit a Watcher was unlikely; to take in a Changeling or some other guildless person was improbable beyond comprehension. When we presented ourselves, therefore, we were met by Servitors whose attitude was at first one of high humor at our joke, then of irritation, finally of scorn. 'Get away,' they told us ultimately. 'Scum! Rabble!'

Avluela said in a grave voice, 'The Prince has granted us lodging here, and you may not refuse us.'

'Away! Away!'

One snaggle-toothed Servitor produced a neural truncheon and brandished it in Gormon's face, passing a foul remark about his guildlessness. Gormon slapped the truncheon from the man's grasp, oblivious to the painful sting, and kicked him in the gut, so that he coiled and fell over, puking. Instantly a throng of neuters came rushing from within the hostelry. Gormon seized another of the Servitors and hurled him into the midst of them, turning them into a muddled mob. Wild shouts and angry cursing cries attracted the attention of a venerable Scribe who waddled to the door, bellowed for silence, and interrogated us. 'That's easily checked,' he said, when Avluela had told the story. To a Servitor he said contemptuously, 'Send a think to the Indexers, fast!'

In time the confusion was untangled and we were admitted. We were given separate but adjoining rooms. I had never known such luxury before, and perhaps never shall again. The rooms were long, high and deep. One entered them through telescopic pits keyed to one's own thermal output, to assure privacy. Lights glowed at the resident's merest nod, for hanging from ceiling globes and nestling in cupolas on the walls were spicules of slave-light from one of the Brightstar worlds, trained through suffering to obey such commands. The windows came and went at the dweller's whim; when not in use, they were concealed by streamers of quasi-sentient outworld gauzes, which not only were decorative in their own right, but which functioned as monitors to produce delightful scents according to requisitioned patterns. The rooms were equipped with individual thinking caps connected to the main memory banks. They likewise had conduits that summoned Servitors, Scribes, Indexers, or Musicians as required. Of course, a man of my own humble guild would not deign to make use of other human beings that way, out of fear of their glowering resentment; but in any case I had little need of them.

I did not ask of Avluela what had occurred in the Prince's palanquin to bring us such bounty. I could well imagine, as could Gormon, whose barely suppressed inner rage was eloquent of his never-admitted love for my pale, slender little Flier.

We settled in. I placed my cart beside the window, draped it with gauzes, and left it in readiness for my next period of Watching. I cleaned my body of grime while entities mounted in the wall sang me to peace. Later I ate. Afterwards Avluela came to me, refreshed and relaxed, and sat beside me in my room as we talked of our experiences. Gormon did not appear for hours. I thought that perhaps he had left this hostelry altogether, finding the atmosphere too rarefied for him, and had sought company among his own guildless kind. But at twilight, Avluela and I walked in the cloistered courtyard of the hostelry and mounted a ramp to watch the stars emerge in Roum's sky, and Gormon was there. With him was a lanky and emaciated man in a Rememberer's shawl; they were talking in low tones.

Gormon nodded to me and said, 'Watcher, meet my new friend.'

The emaciated one fingered his shawl. 'I am the Rememberer Basil,' he intoned, in a voice as thin as a fresco that has been peeled from its wall. 'I have come from Perris to delve into the mysteries of Roum. I shall be here many years.'

'The Rememberer has fine stories to tell,' said Gormon. 'He is among the foremost of his guild. As you approached, he was describing to me the techniques by which the past is revealed. They drive a trench through the strata of Third Cycle deposits, you see, and with vacuum cores they lift the molecules of earth to lay bare the ancient layers.'

'We have found,' Basil said, 'the catacombs of Imperial Roum, and the rubble of the Time of Sweeping, the books inscribed on slivers of white metal, written toward the close of the Second Cycle. All these go to Perris for examination and classification and decipherment; then they return. Does the past interest you, Watcher?'

'To some extent.' I smiled. 'This Changeling here shows much more fascination for it. I sometimes suspect his authenticity. Would you recognize a Rememberer in disguise?'

Basil scrutinized Gormon; he lingered over the bizarre features, the excessively muscular frame. 'He is no Rememberer,' he said at length. 'But I agree that he has antiquarian interests. He has asked me many profound questions.'

'Such as?'

'He wishes to know the origin of Guilds. He asks the name of the genetic surgeon who crafted the first true-breeding Fliers. He wonders why there are Changelings, and if they are truly under the curse of the Will.'

'And do you have answers for these?' I asked.

'For some,' said Basil. 'For some.'

'The origin of guilds?'

'To give structure and meaning to a society that has suffered defeat and destruction,' said the Rememberer. 'At the end of the Second Cycle all was in flux. No man knew his rank nor his purpose. Through our world strode haughtily outworlders who looked upon us all as worthless. It was necessary to establish fixed frames of reference by which one man might know his value beside another. So the first guilds appeared: Dominators, Masters, Merchants, Landholders, Vendors and Servitors. Then came Scribes, Musicians, Clowns and Transporters. Afterwards Indexers

32

became necessary, and then Watchers and Defenders. When the Years of Magic gave us Fliers and Changelings, those guilds were added, and then the guildless ones, the neuters, were produced, so that—'

'But surely the Changelings are guildless too!' said Avluela.

The Rememberer looked at her for the first time. 'Who are you, child?'

'Avluela of the Fliers. I travel with this Watcher and this Changeling.'

Basil said, 'As I have been telling the Changeling here, in the early days his kind was guilded. The guild was dissolved a thousand years ago by the order of the Council of Dominators after an attempt by a disreputable Changeling faction to seize control of the holy places of Jorslem, and since that time Changelings have been guildless, ranking only above neuters.'

'I never knew that,' I said.

'You are no Rememberer,' said Basil smugly. 'It is our craft to uncover the past.'

'True. True.'

'Gormon said, 'And today, how many guilds are there?'

Discomfited, Basil replied vaguely, 'At least a hundred, my friend. Some quite small; some are local. I am concerned only with the original guilds and their immediate successors; what has happened in the past few hundred years is in the province of others. Shall I requisition an information for you?'

'Never mind,' Gormon said. 'It was only an idle question.'

'Your curiosity is well developed,' said the Rememberer.

'I find the world and all it contains extremely fascinating. Is this sinful?'

'It is strange,' said Basil. 'The guildless rarely look beyond their own horizons.'

A Servitor appeared. With a mixture of awe and contempt he genuflected before Avluela and said, 'The Prince has returned. He desires your company in the palace at this time.'

Terror glimmered in Avluela's eyes. But to refuse was inconceivable. 'Shall I come with you?' she asked.

'Please. You must be robed and perfumed. He wishes

33

you to come to him with your wings open, as well.'

Avluela nodded. The Servitor led her away.

We remained on the ramp a while longer; the Rememberer Basil talked of the old days of Roum, and I listened, and Gormon peered into the gathering darkness. Eventually, his throat dry, the Rememberer excused himself and moved solemnly away. A few moments later, in the courtyard below us, a door opened and Avluela emerged, walking as though she were of the guild of Somnambulists, not of Fliers. She was nude under transparent draperies, and her fragile body gleamed ghostly in the starbeams. Her wings were spread and fluttered slowly in a sombre systole and diastole. One Servitor grasped each of her elbows: they seemed to be propelling her toward the palace as though she were but a dreamed facsimile of herself and not a real woman.

'Fly, Avluela, fly,' Gormon growled. 'Escape while you can!'

She disappeared into a side entrance of the palace.

The Changeling looked at me. 'She has sold herself to the Prince to provide lodging for us.'

'So it seems.'

'I could smash down that palace!'

'You love her?'

'It should be obvious.'

'Cure yourself,' I advised. 'You are an unusual man, but still a Flier is not for you. Particularly a Flier who has shared the bed of the Prince of Roum.'

'She goes from my arms to his.'

I was staggered. 'You've known her?'

'More than once,' he said, smiling sadly. 'At the moment of ecstasy her wings thrash like leaves in a storm.'

I gripped the railing of the ramp so that I would not tumble into the courtyard. The stars whirled overhead; the old moon and its two blank-faced consorts leaped and bobbed. I was shaken without fully understanding the cause of my emotion. Was it wrath that Gormon had dared to violate a canon of the law? Was it a manifestation of those pseudo-parental feelings I had toward Avluela? Or was it mere envy of Gormon for daring to commit a sin beyond my capacity, though not beyond my desires?

I said, 'They could burn your brain for that. They could mince your soul. And now you make me an accessory.'

'What of it? That Prince commands, and he gets — but others have been there before him. I had to tell someone.'

'Enough. Enough.'

'Will we see her again?'

'Princes tire quickly of their women. A few days, perhaps a single night — then he will throw her back to us. And perhaps then we shall have to leave this hostelry.' I sighed. 'At least we'll have known it a few nights more than we deserved.'

'Where will you go then?' Gormon asked.

'I will stay in Roum a while.'

'Even if you sleep in the streets? There does not seem to be much demand for Watchers here.'

'I'll manage,' I said. 'Then I may go toward Perris.'

'To learn from the Rememberers?'

'To see Perris. What of you? What do you want in Roum?'

'Avluela.'

'Stop that talk!'

'Very well,' he said, and his smile was bitter. 'But I will stay here until the Prince is through with her. Then she will be mine, and we'll find ways to survive. The guildless are resourceful. They have to be. Maybe we'll scrounge lodgings in Roum awhile, and then follow you to Perris. If you're willing to travel with monsters and faithless Fliers.'

I shrugged. 'We'll see about that when the time comes.'

'Have you ever been in the company if a Changeling before?'

'Not often. Not for long.'

'I'm honored.' He drummed on the parapet. 'Don't cast me off, Watcher. I have a reason for wanting to stay with you.'

'Which is?'

'To see your face on the day your machines tell you that the invasion of Earth has begun.'

I let myself sag forward, shoulders drooping. 'You'll stay with me a long time, then.'

'Don't you believe the invasion is coming?'

'Some day. Not soon.'

Gormon chuckled. 'You're wrong. It's almost here.'

'You don't amuse me.'

'What is it, Watcher? Have you lost your faith? It's been

35

known for a thousand years: another race covets Earth and owns it by treaty, and will some day come to collect. That much was decided at the end of the Second Cycle.'

'I know all that, and I am no Rememberer.' Then I turned to him and spoke words I never thought I would say aloud. 'For twice your lifetime, Changeling, I've listened to the stars and done my Watching. Something done that often loses meaning. Say your own name ten thousand times and it will be an empty sound. I have Watched, and Watched well, and in the dark hours of the night I sometimes think I Watch for nothing, that I have wasted my life. There is a pleasure in Watching, but perhaps there is no real purpose.'

His hand encircled my wrist. 'Your confession is as shocking as mine. Keep your faith, Watcher. The invasion comes!'

'How could you possibly know?'

'The guildless also have their skills.'

The conversation troubled me. I said, 'Is it painful to be guildless?'

'One grows reconciled. And there are certain freedoms to compensate for the lack of status. I may speak freely to all.'

'I notice.'

'I move freely. I am always sure of food and lodging, though the food may be rotten and the lodging poor. Women are attracted to me despite all prohibitions. Because of them, perhaps. I am untroubled by ambitions.'

'Never desire to rise above your rank?'

'Never.'

'You might have been happier as a Rememberer.'

'I am happy now. I can have a Rememberer's pleasures without his responsibility.'

'How smug you are!' I cried. 'To make a virtue of guildlessness!'

'How else does one endure the weight of the Will?' He looked towards the palace. 'The humble rise. The mighty fall. Take this as prophecy, Watcher: that lusty Prince in there will know more of life before summer comes. I'll rip out his eyes for taking Avluela!'

'Strong words. You bubble with treason tonight.'

'Take it as prophecy.'

'You can't get close to him,' I said. Then, irritated for taking his foolishness seriously, I added, 'And why blame him? He only does as princes do. Blame the girl for going to him. She might have refused.'

'And lost her wings. Or died. No, she had no choice. I do!' In a sudden, terrible gesture the Changeling held out thumb and forefinger, double-jointed, long-nailed, and plunged them into imagined eyes. 'Wait,' he said. 'You'll see!'

In the courtyard two Chronomancers appeared, set up the apparatus of their guild, and lit tapers by which to read the shape of tomorrow. A sickly odor of pallid smoke rose to my nostrils. I had now lost further desire to speak with the Changeling.

'It grows late,' I said. 'I need rest, and soon I must do my Watching.'

'Watch carefully,' Gormon told me.

5

AT NIGHT in my chamber I performed my fourth and last Watch of that long day, and for the first time in my life I detected an anomaly. I could not interpret it. It was an obscure sensation, a mingling of tastes and sounds, a feeling of being in contact with some colossal mass. Worried, I clung to my instruments far longer than usual, but perceived no more clearly at the end of my seance than at its commencement.

Afterward I wondered about my obligations.

Watchers are trained from childhood to be swift to sound the alarm; and the alarm must be sounded when the Watcher judges the world in peril. Was I now obliged to notify the Defenders? Four times in my life the alarm had been given, on each occasion in error; and each Watcher who had thus touched off a false mobilization had suffered a fearful loss of status. One had contributed his brain to the memory banks; one had become a neuter out of shame; one had smashed his instruments and gone to live among the guildless; and one, vainly attempting to continue in his profession, had discovered himself mocked by all his comrades. I saw no virtue in scorning one who had delivered a false alarm, for was it not preferable for a Watcher to cry out too soon than not at all? But those were the customs of our guild, and I was constrained by them.

I evaluated my position and decided that I did not have valid grounds for an alarm.

I reflected that Gormon had placed suggestive ideas in my mind that evening. I might possibly be reacting only to his jeering talk of imminent invasions.

I could not act. I dared not jeopardize my standing by hasty outcry. I mistrusted my own emotional state.

I gave no alarm.

Seething, confused, my soul boiling, I closed my cart and let myself sink into a drugged sleep.

At dawn I woke and rushed to the window, expecting to

find invaders in the streets. But all was still; a winter grayness hung over the courtyard, and sleepy Servitors pushed passive neuters about. Uneasily I did my first Watching of the day, and to my relief the strangeness of the night before did not return, although I had it in mind that my sensitivity is always greater at night than upon arising.

I ate and went to the courtyard. Gormon and Avluela were already there. She looked fatigued and downcast, depleted by her night with the Prince of Roum, but I said nothing to her about it. Gormon, slouching disdainfully against a wall embellished with the shells of radiant mollusks, said to me, 'Did your Watching go well?'

'Well enough.'

'What of the day?'

'Out to roam Roum,' I said. 'Will you come? Avluela? Gormon?'

'Surely,' he said, and she gave a faint nod; and, like the tourists we were, we set off to inspect the splendid city of Roum.

Gormon acted as our guide to the jumbled pasts of Roum, belying his claim never to have been here before. As well as any Rememberer he described the things we saw as we walked the winding streets. All the scattered levels of thousands of years were exposed. We saw the power domes of the Second Cycle, and the Colosseum where at an unimaginably early date man and beast contended like jungle creatures. In the broken hull of that building of horrors Gormon told us of the savagery of that unimaginably ancient time. 'They fought,' he said, 'naked before huge throngs. With bare hands men challenged beasts called lions, great hairy cats with swollen heads; and when the lion lay in its gore, the victor turned to the Prince of Roum and asked to be pardoned for whatever crime it was that had cast him into the arena. And if he had fought well, the Prince made a gesture with his hand, and the man was freed.' Gormon made the gesture for us: a thumb upraised and jerked backward over the right shoulder several times. 'But if the man had shown cowardice, or if the lion had distinguished itself in the manner of its dying, the Prince made another gesture, and the man was condemned to be slain by a second beast.' Gormon showed us that gesture too: the middle finger jutting upward from a clenched fist and lifted in a short sharp thrust.

'How are these things known?' Avluela asked, but Gormon pretended not to hear her.

We saw the line of fusion-pylons built early in the Third Cycle to draw energy from the world's core; they were still functioning, although stained and corroded. We saw the shattered stump of a Second Cycle weather machine, still a mighty column at least twenty men high. We saw a hill on which white marble relics of First Cycle Roum sprouted like pale clumps of winter deathflowers. Penetrating toward the inner part of the city, we came upon the embankment of defensive amplifiers waiting in readiness to hurl the full impact of the Will against invaders. We viewed a market where visitors from the stars haggled with peasants for excavated fragments of antiquity. Gormon strode into the crowd and made several purchases. We came to a flesh-house for travelers from afar, where one could buy anything from quasi-life to mounds of passion-ice. We ate at a small restaurant by the edge of the River Tver, where guildless ones were served without ceremony, and at Gormon's insistence we dined on mounds of a soft doughy substance and drank a tart yellow wine, local specialities.

Afterward we passed through a covered arcade in whose many aisles plump Vendors peddled star-goods, costly trinkets from Afreek, and the flimsy constructs of the local Manufactories. Just beyond we emerged in a plaza that contained a fountain in the shape of a boat, and to the rear of this rose a flight of cracked and battered stone-stairs ascending to a zone of rubble and weeds. Gormon beckoned, and we scrambled into this dismal area, then passed rapidly through it to a place where a sumptuous palace, by its looks early Second Cycle or even First, brooded over a sloping vegetated hill.

'They say this is the center of the world,' Gormon declared. 'In Jorslem one finds another place that also claims the honor. They mark the spot here by a map.'

'How can the world have one center,' Avluela asked, 'when it is round?'

Gormon laughed. We went in. Within, in wintry darkness, there stood a colossal jeweled globe lit by some inner glow.

40

'Here is your world,' said Gormon, gesturing grandly.

'Oh!' Avluela gasped. 'Everything! Everything is here!'

The map was a masterpiece of craftsmanship. It showed natural contours and elevations, its seas seemed deep liquid pools, its deserts were so parched as to make thirst spring in one's mouth, its cities swirled with vigor and life. I beheld the continents, Eyrop, Afreek, Ais, Stralya. I saw the vastness of Earth Ocean. I traversed the golden span of Land Bridge, which I had crossed so toilfully on foot not long before. Avluela rushed forward and pointed to Roum, to Agupt, to Jorslem, to Perris. She tapped the globe at the high mountains north of Hind and said softly, 'This is where I was born, where the ice lives, where the mountains touch the moons. Here is where the Fliers have their kingdom.' She ran a finger westward toward Fars and beyond it into the terrible Arban Desert, and on to Agupt. 'This is where I flew. By night, when I left my girlhood. We all must fly, and I flew here. A hundred times I thought I would die. Here, here in the desert, sand in my throat as I flew, sand beating against my wings – I was forced down, I lay naked on the hot sand for days, and another Flier saw me, he came down to me and pitied me, and lifted me up, and when I was aloft my strength returned, and we flew on toward Agupt. And he died over the sea, his life stopped though he was young and strong, and he fell down into the sea, and I flew down to be with him, and the water was hot even at night. I drifted and morning came, and I saw the living stones growing like trees in the water, and the fish of many colors, and they came to him and pecked at his flesh as he floated with his wings outspread on the water, and I left him, I thrust him down to rest there, and I rose, and I flew on to Agupt, alone, frightened, and there I met you, Watcher.' Timidly she smiled at me. 'Show us the place where you were young, Watcher.'

Painfully, for I was suddenly stiff at the knees, I hobbled to the far side of the globe. Avluela followed me; Gormon hung back, as though not interested at all. I pointed to the scattered islands rising in two long strips from Earth Ocean – the remnants of the Lost Continents.

'Here,' I said, indicating my native island in the west. 'I was born here.'

'So far away!' Avluela cried.

41

'And so long ago,' I said. 'In the middle of the Second Cycle, it sometimes seems to me.'

'No! That is not possible!' But she looked at me as though it might have been true that I was thousands of years old.

I smiled and touched her satiny cheek. 'It only seems that way to me,' I said.

'When did you leave home?'

'When I was twice your age,' I said. 'I came first to here —' I indicated the eastern group of islands. 'I spent a dozen years as a Watcher on Palash. Then the Will moved me to cross Earth Ocean to Afreek. I came. I lived awhile in the hot countries. I went on to Agupt. I met a certain small Flier.' Falling silent, I looked a long while at the islands that had been my home, and within my mind my image changed from the gaunt and eroded thing I now had become, and I saw myself young and well-fleshed, climbing the green mountains and swimming in the chill sea, doing my Watching at the rim of a white beach hammered by surf.

While I brooded Avluela turned away from me to Gormon and said, 'Now you. Show us where you came from, Changeling!'

Gormon shrugged. 'The place does not appear to be on this globe.'

'But that's *impossible!*'

'Is it?' he asked.

She pressed him, but he evaded her, and we passed through a side exit and into the streets of Roum.

I was growing tired, but Avluela hungered for this city and wished to devour it all in an afternoon, and so we went on through a maze of interlocking streets, through a zone of sparkling mansions of Masters and Merchants, and through a foul den of Servitors and Vendors that extended into subterranean catacombs, and to a place where Clowns and Musicians resorted, and to another where the guild of Somnambulists offered its doubtful wares. A bloated female Somnambulist begged us to come inside and buy the truth that comes with trances, and Avluela urged us to go, but Gormon shook his head and I smiled, and we moved on. Now we were at the edge of a park close to the city's core. Here the citizens of Roum promenaded with an energy rarely seen in hot Agupt, and we joined the parade.

'Look there!' Avluela said. 'How bright it is!'

She pointed toward the shining arc of a dimensional sphere enclosing some relic of the ancient city; shading my eyes, I could make out a weathered stone wall within, and a knot of people. Gormon said, 'It is the Mouth of Truth.'

'What is that?' Avluela asked.

'Come. See.'

A line progressed into the sphere. We joined it and soon were at the tip of the interior, peering at the timeless region just across the threshold. Why this relic and so few others had been accorded such special protection I did not know, and I asked Gormon, whose knowledge was so unaccountably as profound as any Rememberer's, and he replied, 'Because this is the realm of certainty, where what one says is absolutely congruent with what actually is the case.'

'I don't understand,' said Avluela.

'It is impossible to lie in this place,' Gormon told her. 'Can you imagine any relic more worthy of protection?' He stepped across the entry duct, blurring as he did so, and I followed him quickly within. Avluela hesitated. It was a long moment before she entered; pausing a moment on the very threshold, she seemed buffeted by the wind that blew along the line of demarcation between the outer world and the pocket universe in which we stood.

An inner compartment held the Mouth of Truth itself. The line extended toward it, and a solemn Indexer was controlling the flow of entry to the tabernacle. It was a while before we three were permitted to go in. We found ourselves before the ferocious head of a monster in high relief, affixed to an ancient wall pockmarked by time. The monster's jaws gaped; the open mouth was a dark and sinister hole. Gormon nodded, inspecting it, as though he seemed pleased to find it exactly as he had thought it would be.

'What do we do?' Avluela asked.

Gormon said, 'Watcher, put your right hand into the Mouth of Truth.'

Frowning, I complied.

'Now,' said Gormon, 'one of us asks a question. You must answer it. If you speak anything but the truth, the mouth will close and sever your hand.'

'No!' Avluela cried.

I stared uneasily at the stone jaws rimming my wrist. A

43

Watcher without both his hands is a man without a craft; in Second Cycle days one might have obtained a prosthesis more artful than one's original hand, but the Second Cycle had long ago been concluded, and such niceties were not to be purchased on Earth nowadays.

'How is such a thing possible?' I asked.

'The Will is unusually strong in these precincts,' Gormon replied. 'It distinguishes sternly between truth and untruth. To the rear of this wall sleeps a trio of Somnambulists through whom the Will speaks, and they control the Mouth. Do you fear the Will, Watcher?'

' I fear my own tongue.'

'Be brave. Never has a lie been told before this wall. Never has a hand been lost.'

'Go ahead, then,' I said. 'Who will ask me a question?'

'I,' said Gormon. 'Tell me, Watcher: all pretense aside, would you say that a life spent in Watching has been a life spent wisely?'

I was silent a long moment, rotating my thoughts, eyeing the jaws.

At length I said, 'To devote oneself to vigilance on behalf of one's fellow man is perhaps the noblest purpose one can serve.'

'Careful!' Gormon cried in alarm.

'I am not finished,' I said.

'Go on.'

'But to devote oneself to vigilance when the enemy is an imaginary one is idle, and to congratulate oneself for looking long and well for a foe that is not coming is foolish and sinful. My life has been a waste.'

The jaws of the Mouth of Truth did not quiver.

I removed my hand. I stared at it as though it had newly sprouted from my wrist. I felt suddenly several cycles old. Avluela, her eyes wide, her hands to her lips, seemed shocked by what I had said. My own words appeared to hang congealed in the air before the hideous idol.

'Spoken honestly,' said Gormon, 'although without much mercy for yourself. You judge yourself too harshly, Watcher.'

'I spoke to save my hand,' I said. 'Would you have had me lie?'

44

He smiled. To Avluela the Changeling said, 'Now it's your turn.'

Visibly frightened, the little Flier approached the Mouth. Her dainty hand trembled as she inserted it between the slabs of cold stone. I fought back an urge to rush toward her and pull her free of that devilish grimacing head.

'Who will question her? I asked.

'I,' said Gormon.

Avluela's wings stirred faintly beneath her garments. Her face grew pale; her nostrils flickered; her upper lip slid over the lower one. She stood slouched against the wall and stared in horror at the termination of her arm. Outside the chamber vague faces peered at us; lips moved in what no doubt were expressions of impatience over our lengthy visit to the Mouth; but we heard nothing. The atmosphere around us was warm and clammy, with a musty tang like that which would come from a well that was driven through the structure of Time.

Gormon said slowly, 'This night past you allowed your body to be possessed by the Prince of Roum. Before that, you granted yourself to the Changeling Gormon, although such liaisons are forbidden by custom and law. Much prior to that you were the mate of a Flier, now deceased. You may have had other men, but I know nothing of them, and for the purposes of my question they are not relevant. Tell me this, Avluela: which of the three gave you the most intense physical pleasure, which of the three aroused your deepest emotions, and which of the three would you choose as a mate?'

I wanted to protest that the Changeling had asked her three questions, not one, and so had taken unfair advantage. But I had no chance to speak, because Avluela replied unfalteringly, hand wedged deep into the Mouth of Truth, 'The Prince of Roum gave me greater pleasure of the body than I had ever known before, but he is cold and cruel, and I despise him. My dead Flier I loved more deeply than any person before or since, but he was weak, and I would not have wanted a weakling as a mate. You, Gormon, seem almost a stranger to me even now, and I feel that I know neither your body nor your soul, and yet, though the gulf between us is wide, it is you with whom I would spend my days to come.'

She drew her hand from the Mouth of Truth.

'Well spoken!' said Gormon, though the accuracy of her words had clearly wounded as well as pleased him. 'Suddenly you find eloquence, eh, when the circumstances demand it. And now the turn is mine to risk my hand.'

He neared the Mouth. I said, 'You have asked the first two questions. Do you wish to finish the job and ask the third as well?'

'Hardly,' he said. He made a negligent gesture with his free hand. 'Put your heads together and agree on a joint question.'

Avluela and I conferred. With uncharacteristic forwardness she proposed a question; and since it was the one I would have asked, I accepted it and told her to ask it.

She said, 'When we stood before the globe of the world, Gormon, I asked you to show me the place where you were born, and you said you were unable to find it on the map. That seemed most strange. Tell me now: are you what you say you are, a Changeling who wanders the world?'

He replied. 'I am not.'

In a sense he had satisfied the question as Avluela had phrased it; but it went without saying that his reply was inadequate, and he kept his hand in the Mouth of Truth as he continued, 'I did not show my birthplace to you on the globe because I was born nowhere on this globe, but on a world of a star I must not name. I am no Changeling in your meaning of the word, though by some definitions I am, for my body is somewhat disguised, and on my own world I wear a different flesh. I have lived here ten years.'

'What was your purpose in coming to Earth?' I asked.

'I am obliged only to answer one question,' said Gormon. Then he smiled. 'But I give you the answer anyway: I was sent to Earth in the capacity of a military observer, to prepare the way for the invasion for which you have Watched so long and in which you have ceased to believe, and which will be upon you in a matter now of some hours.'

'Lies!' I bellowed. '*Lies!*'

Gormon laughed. And drew his hand from the Mouth of Truth, intact, unharmed.

6

NUMB with confusion, I fled with my cart of instruments from that gleaming sphere and emerged into a street suddenly cold and dark. Night had come with winter's swiftness; it was almost the ninth hour, and almost the time for me to Watch once more.

Gormon's mockery thundered in my brain. He had arranged everything: he had maneuvered us in to the Mouth of Truth; he had wrung a confession of lost faith from me and a confession of a different sort from Avluela; he had mercilessly volunteered information he need not have revealed, spoken words calculated to split me to the core.

Was the Mouth of Truth a fraud? Could Gormon lie and emerge unscathed?

Never since I first took up my tasks had I Watched at anything but the appointed hours. This was a time of crumbling realities; I could not wait for the ninth hour to come round; crouching in the windy street, I opened my cart, readied my equipment, and sank like a diver into Watchfulness.

My amplified consciousness roared toward the stars.

Godlike I roamed infinity. I felt the rush of the solar wind, but I was no Flier to be hurled to destruction by that pressure, and I soared past it, beyond the reach of those angry particles of light, into the blackness at the edge of the sun's dominion. Down upon me there beat a different pressure.

Starships coming near.

Not the tourist lines bringing sightseers to gape at our diminished world. Not the registered mercantile transport vessels, nor the scoopships that collect the interstellar vapors, nor the resort craft on their hyperbolic orbits.

These were military craft, dark, alien, menacing. I could not tell their number; I knew only that they sped Earthward at many lights, nudging a cone of deflected energies before them; and it was that cone that I had sensed, that I had

47

felt also the night before, booming into my mind through my instruments, engulfing me like a cube of crystal through which stress patterns play and shine.

All my life I had watched for this.

I had been trained to sense it. I had prayed that I never would sense it, and then in my emptiness I had prayed that I *would* sense it, and then I had ceased to believe in it. And then by grace of the Changeling Gormon, I had sensed it after all, Watching ahead of my hour, crouching in a cold Roumish street just outside the Mouth of Truth.

In his training, a Watcher is instructed to break from his Watchfulness as soon as his observations are confirmed by a careful check, so that he can sound the alarm. Obediently I made my check by shifting from one channel to another to another, triangulating and still picking up that foreboding sensation of titanic force rushing upon Earth at unimaginable speed.

Either I was deceived, or the invasion was come. But I could not shake from my trance to give the alarm.

Lingeringly, lovingly, I drank in the sensory data for what seemed like hours. I fondled my equipment; I drained from it the total affirmation of faith that my readings gave me. Dimly I warned myself that I was wasting vital time, that it was my duty to leave this lewd caressing of destiny to summon the Defenders.

And at last I burst free from Watchfulness and returned to the world I was guarding.

Avluela was beside me; she was dazed, terrified, her knuckles to her teeth, her eyes blank.

'Watcher! Watcher, do you hear me? What's happening? What's going to happen?'

'The invasion,' I said. 'How long was I under?'

'About half a minute. I don't know. Your eyes were closed. I thought you were dead.'

'Gormon was speaking the truth! The *invasion* is almost here. Where is he? Where did he go?'

'He vanished as we came away from that place with the Mouth,' Avluela whispered. 'Watcher, I'm frightened. I feel everything collapsing. I have to fly – I can't stay down here now!'

'Wait,' I said, clutching at her and missing her arm. 'Don't go now. First I have to give the alarm, and then—'

But she was already stripping off her clothing. Bare to the waist, her pale body gleamed in the evening light, while about us people were rushing to and fro in ignorance of all that was about to occur. I wanted to keep Avluela beside me, but I could delay no longer in giving the alarm, and I turned away from her, back to my care.

As though caught up in a dream born of overripe longings I reached for the node that I had never used, the one that would send forth a planetwide alert to the Defenders.

Had the alarm already been given? Had some other Watcher sensed what I had sensed, and less paralyzed by bewilderment and doubt, performed a Watcher's final task?

No. No. For then I would be hearing the sirens' shriek reverberating from the orbiting loudspeakers above the city.

I touched the node. From the corner of my eye I saw Avluela, free of her encumbrances now, kneeling to say her words, filling her tender wings with strength. In a moment she would be in the air, beyond my grasp.

With a single swift tug I activated the alarm.

In that instant I became aware of a burly figure striding toward us. Gormon, I thought: and as I rose from my equipment I reached out to him; I wanted to seize him and hold him fast. But he who approached was not Gormon but some officious dough-faced Servitor who said to Avluela, 'Go easy, Flier, let your wings drop. The Prince of Roum sends me to bring you to his presence.'

He grappled with her. Her little breasts heaved; her eyes flashed anger at him.

'Let go of me! I'm going to fly!'

'The Prince of Roum summons you,' the Servitor said, enclosing her in his heavy arms.

'The Prince of Roum will have other distractions tonight,' I said. 'He'll have no need of her.'

As I spoke the sirens began to sing from the skies.

The Servitor released her. His mouth worked noiselessly for an instant; he made one of the protective gestures of the Will; he looked skyward and grunted, 'The alarm! Who gave the alarm? You, old Watcher?'

Figures rushed about insanely in the streets.

Avluela, freed, sped past me – on foot, her wings but half-furled – and was swallowed up in the surging throng.

Over the terrifying sound of the sirens came booming messages from the public annunciators, giving instructions for defense and safety. A lanky man with the mark of the guild of Defenders upon his cheek rushed to me, shouted words too incoherent to be understood, and sped on down the street. The world seemed to have gone mad.

Only I remained calm. I looked to the skies, half-expecting to see the invaders' black ships already hovering above the towers of Roum. But I saw nothing except the hovering nightlights and the other objects one might expect overhead.

'Gormon?' I called. 'Avluela?'

I was alone.

A strange emptiness swept over me. I had given the alarm; the invaders were on their way; I had lost my occupation. There was no need of Watchers now. Almost lovingly I touched the worn cart that had been my companion for so many years. I ran my fingers over its stained and pitted instruments; and then I looked away, abandoning it, and went down the dark streets cartless, burdenless, a man whose life had found and lost meaning in the same instant. And about me raged chaos.

7

IT was understood that when the moment of Earth's final battle arrived, all guilds would be mobilized, the Watchers alone exempted. We who had manned the perimeter of defense for so long had no part in the strategy of combat; we were discharged by the giving of a true alarm. Now it was the time of the guild of Defenders to show its capabilities. They had planned for half a cycle what they would do in time of war. What plans would they call forth now? What deeds would they direct?

My only concern was to return to the royal hostelry and wait out the crisis. It was hopeless to think of finding Avluela, and I pummeled myself savagely for having let her slip away, naked and without a protector, in that confused moment. Where would she go? Who would shield her?

A fellow Watcher, pulling his cart madly along, nearly collided with me. 'Careful!' I snapped. He looked up, breathless, stunned. 'Is it true?' he asked. 'The alarm?'

'Can't you hear?'

'But is it real?'

I pointed to his cart. 'You know how to find that out.'

'They say the man who gave the alarm was drunk, an old fool who was turned away from the inn yesterday.'

'It could be so,' I admitted.

'But if the alarm is real—!'

Smiling, I said, 'If it is, now we all may rest. Good day to you, Watcher.'

'Your cart! Where's your cart?' he shouted at me.

But I had moved past him, toward the mighty carven stone pillar of some relic of Imperial Roum.

Ancient images were carved on that pillar; battles and victories, foreign monarchs marched in the chains of disgrace through the streets of Roum, triumphant eagles celebrating imperial grandeur. In my strange new calmness I stood awhile before the column of stone and admired its elegant engravings. Toward me rushed a frenzied figure whom I recognized as the Rememberer Basil; I hailed him, saying, 'How timely you come! Do me the kindness of explaining these images, Rememberer. They fascinate me, and my curiosity is aroused.'

'Are you insane? Can't you hear the alarm?'

'I gave the alarm, Rememberer.'

'Flee, then! Invaders come! We must fight!'

'Not I. Basil. Now my time is over. Tell me of these images. These beaten kings, these broken emperors. Surely a man of your years will not be doing battle.'

'All are mobilized now!'

'All but Watchers,' I said. 'Take a moment. Yearning for the past is born in me. Gormon has vanished; be my guide to these lost cycles.'

The Rememberer shook his head wildly, circled around me, and tried to get away. Hoping to seize his skinny arm and pin him to the spot, I made a lunge at him, but he eluded me and I caught only his dark shawl, which pulled free and came loose in my hands. Then he was gone, his spindly limbs pumping madly as he fled down the street and left my view. I shrugged and examined the shawl I had so unexpectedly acquired. It was shot through with glimmering threads of metal arranged in intricate patterns that teased the eye: it seemed to me that each strand disappeared into the weave of the fabric, only to appear at some improbable point, like the lineage of dynasties unexpectedly revived in distant cities. The workmanship was superb. Idly I draped the shawl about my shoulders.

I walked on.

My legs, which had been on the verge of failing me earlier in the day, now served me well. With renewed youthfulness I made my way through the chaotic city, finding no difficulties in choosing my route. I headed for the river, then crossed it and, on the Tver's far side, sought the palace of the Prince. The night had deepened, for most lights were extinguished under the mobilization orders; and from time to time a dull boom signaled the explosion of a screening bomb overhead, liberating clouds of murk that shielded the city from most forms of long-range scrutiny. There were fewer pedestrians in the streets. The sirens still cried out. Atop the buildings the defense installations were going into action; I heard the bleeping sounds of repellors warming

52

up, and I saw long spidery arms of amplification booms swinging from tower to tower as they linked for maximum output. I had no doubt now that the invasion actually was coming. My own instruments might have been fouled by inner confusion, but they would not have proceeded thus far with the mobilization if the initial report had not been confirmed by the findings of hundreds of other members of my guild.

As I neared the palace a pair of breathless Rememberers sped toward me, their shawls flapping behind them. They called to me in words I did not comprehend – some code of their guild, I realized, recollecting that I wore Basil's shawl. I could not reply, and they rushed upon me, still gabbling; and switching to the language of ordinary men they said, 'What is the matter with you? To your post! We must record! We must comment! We must observe!'

'You mistake me,' I said mildly. 'I keep this shawl only for your brother Basil, who left it in my care. I have no post to guard at this time.'

'A Watcher,' they cried in unison, and cursed me separately, and ran on. I laughed and went to the palace.

Its gates stood open. The neuters who had guarded the outer portals had gone, as were the two Indexers who had stood just within the door. The beggars that had thronged the vast plaza had jostled their way into the building itself to seek shelter; this had awakened the anger of the licensed hereditary mendicants whose customary stations were in that part of the building, and they had fallen upon the inflowing refugees with fury and unexpected strength. I saw cripples lashing out with their crutches held as clubs; I saw blind men landing blows with suspicious accuracy; meek penitents were wielding a variety of weapons ranging from stilettos to sonic pistols. Holding myself aloof from this shameless spectacle, I penetrated to the inner recesses of the palace and peered into chapels where I saw Pilgrims beseeching the blessings of the Will, and Communicants desperately seeking spiritual guidance as to the outcome of the coming conflict.

Abruptly I heard the blare of trumpets and cries of, 'Make way! Make way!'

A file of sturdy Servitors marched into the palace, striding toward the Prince's chambers in the apse. Several of them held a struggling, kicking, frantic figure with half-unfolded wings: Avluela! I called out to her, but my voice died in the din, nor could I reach her. The Servitors shoved me aside. The procession vanished into the princely chambers. I caught a final glimpse of the little Flier, pale and small in the grip of her captors, and then she was gone once more.

I seized a bumbling neuter who had been moving uncertainly in the wake of the Servitors.

'That Flier! Why was she brought here?'

'Ha – he – they—'

'Tell me!'

'The Prince – his woman – in his chariot – he – he – they – the invaders—'

I pushed the flabby creature aside and rushed toward the apse. A brazen wall ten times my own height confronted me. I pounded on it. 'Avluela!' I shouted hoarsely. '*Av . . . lu . . . ela . . . !*'

I was neither thrust away nor admitted. I was ignored. The bedlam at the western doors of the palace had extended itself now to the nave and aisles, and as the ragged beggars boiled toward me I executed a quick turn and found myself passing through one of the side doors of the palace.

Suspended and passive, I stood in the courtyard that led to the royal hostelry. A strange electricity crackled in the air. I assumed it was an emanation from one of Roum's defense installations, some kind of beam designed to screen the city from attack. But an instant later I realized that it presaged the actual arrival of the invaders.

Starships blazed in the heavens.

When I had perceived them in my Watching they had appeared black against the infinite blackness, but now they burned with the radiance of suns. A stream of bright, hard, jewel-like globes bedecked the sky; they were ranged side by side, stretching from east to west in a continuous band, filling all the celestial arch, and as they erupted simultaneously into being it seemed to me that I heard the crash and throb of an invisible symphony heralding the arrival of the conquerors of Earth.

I do not know how far above me the starships were, nor how many of them hovered there, not any of the details of their design. I know only that in sudden massive majesty

54

they were there, and that if I had been a Defender my soul would have withered instantly at the sight.

Across the heavens shot light of many hues. The battle had been joined. I could not comprehend the actions of our warriors, and I was equally baffled by the maneuvers of those who had come to take possession of our history-crusted but time-diminished planet. To my shame I felt not only out of the struggle but above the struggle, as though this was no quarrel of mine. I wanted Avluela beside me, and she was somewhere within the depths of the palace of the Prince of Roum. Even Gormon would have been a comfort now, Gormon the Changeling, Gormon the spy, Gormon the monstrous betrayer of our world.

Gigantic amplified voices bellowed, 'Make way for the Prince of Roum! The Prince of Roum leads the Defenders in the battle for the fatherworld!'

From the palace emerged a shining vehicle the shape of a teardrop, in whose bright-metaled roof a transparent sheet had been mounted so that all the populance could see and take heart in the presence of the ruler. At the controls of the vehicle sat the Prince of Roum, proudly erect, his cruel, youthful features fixed in harsh determination; and beside him, robed like an empress, I beheld the slight figure of the Flier Avluela. She seemed in a trance.

The royal chariot soared upward and was lost in the darkness.

It seemed to me that a second vehicle appeared and followed its path, and that the Prince's reappeared, and that the two flew in tight circles, apparently locked in combat. Clouds of blue sparks wrapped both chariots now; and then they swung high and far and were lost to me behind one of the hills of Roum.

Was the battle now raging all over the planet? Was Perris in jeopardy, and holy Jorslem, and even the sleepy isles of the Lost Continents? Did starships hover everywhere? I did not know. I perceived events in only one small segment of the sky over Roum, and even there my awareness of what was taking place was dim, uncertain, and ill-informed. There were momentary flashes of light in which I saw battalions of Fliers streaming across the sky; and then darkness returned as though a velvet shroud had been hurled over the city. I saw the great machines of

55

our defense firing in fitful bursts from the tops of our towers; and yet I saw the starships untouched, unharmed, unmoved above. The courtyard in which I stood was deserted, but in the distance I heard voices, full of fear and foreboding, shouting in tinny tones that might have been the screeching of birds. Occasionally there came a booming sound that rocked all the city. Once a platoon of Somnambulists was driven past where I was; in the plaza fronting the palace I observed what appeared to be an array of Clowns unfolding some sort of sparkling netting of a military look; by one flash of lightning I was able to see a trio of Rememberers making copious notes of all that elapsed as they soared aloft on the gravity plate. It seemed – I was not sure – that the vehicle of the Prince of Roum returned, speeding across the sky with its pursuer clinging close. 'Avluela,' I whispered, as the twin dots of light left my sight. Were the starships disgorging troops? Did colossal pylons of force spiral down from those orbiting brightnesses to touch the surface of the Earth? Why had the Prince seized Avluela? Where was Gormon? What were our Defenders doing? Why were the enemy ships not blasted from the sky?

Rooted to the ancient cobbles of the courtyard, I observed the cosmic battle in total lack of understanding throughout the long night.

Dawn came. Strands of pale light looped from tower to tower. I touched fingers to my eyes, realizing that I must have slept while standing. Perhaps I should apply for membership in the guild of Somnambulists, I told myself lightly. I put my hands to the Rememberer's shawl about my shoulders and wondered how I managed to acquire it, and the answer came.

I looked toward the sky.

The alien starships were gone. I saw only the ordinary morning sky, gray with pinkness breaking through. I felt the jolt of compulsion and looked about for my cart, and reminded myself that I need do no more Watching, and I felt more empty than one would ordinarily feel at such an hour.

Was the battle over?

Had the enemy been vanquished?

Were the ships of the invaders blasted from the sky and lying in charred ruin outside Roum?

All was silent. I heard no more celestial symphonies. Then out of the eerie stillness there came a new sound, a rumbling noise as of wheeled vehicles passing through the streets of the city. And the invisible Musicians played one final note, deep and resonant, which trailed away jaggedly as though every string had been broken at once.

Over the speakers used for public announcements came puiet words.

'Roum is fallen. Roum is fallen.'

8

THE royal hostelry was untended. Neuters and members of the servant guilds all had fled. Defenders, Masters, and Dominators must have perished honorably in combat. Basil the Rememberer was nowhere about; likewise none of his brethren. I went to my room, cleansed and refreshed and fed myself, gathered my few possessions, and bade farewell to the luxuries I had known so briefly. I regretted that I had had such a short time to visit Roum; but at least Gormon had been a most excellent guide, and I had seen a great deal.

Now I proposed to move on.

It did not seem prudent to remain in a conquered city. My room's thinking cap did not respond to my queries, and so I did not know what the extent of the defeat was, here or in other regions, but it was evident to me that Roum at least had passed from human control, and I wished to depart quickly. I weighed the thought of going to Jorslem, as that tall pilgrim had suggested upon my entry into Roum; but then I reflected and chose a westward route, toward Perris, which not only was closer but held the headquarters of the Rememberers. My own occupation had been destroyed; but on this first morning of Earth's conquest I felt a sudden powerful and strange yearning to offer myself humbly to the Rememberers and seek with them knowledge of our more glittering yesterdays.

At midday I left the hostelry. I walked first to the palace, which still stood open. The beggars lay strewn about, some drugged, some sleeping, most dead; from the crude manner of their death I saw that they must have slain one another in their panic and frenzy. A despondent-looking Indexer squatted beside the three skulls of the interrogation fixture in the chapel. As I entered he said, 'No use. The brains do not reply.'

'How goes it with the Prince of Roum?'

'Dead. The invaders shot him from the sky.'

'A young Flier rode beside him. What do you know of her?'

'Nothing. Dead, I suppose.'

'And the city?'

'Fallen. Invaders are everywhere.'

'Killing?'

'Not even looting,' the Indexer said. 'They are most gentle. They have *collected* us.'

'In Roum alone, or everywhere?'

The man shrugged. He began to rock rhythmically back and forth. I let him be, and walked deeper into the palace. To my surprise, the imperial chambers of the Prince were unsealed. I went within; I was awed by the sumptuous luxury of the hangings, the draperies, the lights, the furnishings. I passed from room to room, coming at last to the royal bed, whose coverlet was the flesh of a colossal bivalve of the planet of another star, and as the shell yawned for me I touched the infinitely soft fabric under which the Prince of Roum had lain, and I recalled that Avluela too had lain here, and if I had been a younger man I would have wept.

I left the palace and slowly crossed the plaza to begin my journey toward Perris.

As I departed I had my first glimpse of our conquerors. A vehicle of alien design drew up at the plaza's rim and perhaps a dozen figures emerged. They might almost have been human. They were tall and broad, deep-chested, as Gormon had been, and only the extreme length of their arms marked them instantly as alien. Their skins were of strange texture, and if I had been closer I suspect I would have seen eyes and lips and nostrils that were not of a human design. Taking no notice of me, they crossed the plaza, walking in a curiously loose-jointed loping way that reminded me irresistibly of Gormon's stride, and entered the Palace. They seemed neither swaggering nor belligerent.

Sightseers. Majestic Roum once more exerted its magnetism upon strangers.

Leaving our new masters to their amusement, I walked off, toward the outskirts of the city. The bleakness of eternal winter crept into my soul. I wondered: did I feel sorrow that Roum had fallen? Or did I mourn the loss of Avluela? Or was it only that I now had missed three successive Watchings, and like an addict I was experiencing the pangs of withdrawal?

It was all of these that pained me, I decided. But mostly the last.

No one was abroad in the city as I made for the gates. Fear of the new masters kept the Roumish in hiding, I supposed. From time to time one of the alien vehicles hummed past, but I was unmolested. I came to the city's western gate in the late afternoon. It was open, revealing to me a gentle rising hill on whose breast rose trees with dark green crowns. I passed through and saw, a short distance beyond the gate, the figure of a Pilgrim who was shuffling slowly away from the city.

I overtook him easily.

His faltering, uncertain walk seemed strange to me, for not even his thick brown robes could hide the strength and youth of his body; he stood erect, his shoulders square and his back straight, and yet he walked with the hesitating, trembling step of an old man. When I drew abreast of him and peered under his hood I understood, for affixed to the bronze mask all Pilgrims wear was a reverberator, such as is used by blind men to warn them of obstacles and hazards. He became aware of me and said, 'I am a sightless Pilgrim. I pray you do not molest me.'

It was not a Pilgrim's voice. It was a strong and harsh and imperious voice.

I replied, 'I molest no one. I am a Watcher who has lost his occupation this night past.'

'Many occupations were lost this night past, Watcher.'

'Surely not a Pilgrim's.'

'No,' he said. 'Not a Pilgrim's.'

'Where are you bound?'

'Away from Roum.'

'No particular destination?'

'No,' the Pilgrim said. 'None. I will wander.'

'Perhaps we should wander together,' I said, for it is accounted good luck to travel with a Pilgrim, and, shorn of my Flier and my Changeling, I would otherwise have traveled alone. 'My destination is Perris. Will you come?'

'There as well as anywhere else,' he said bitterly. 'Yes. We will go to Perris together. But what business does a Watcher have there?'

'A watcher has no business anywhere. I go to Perris to offer myself in service to the Rememberers.'

'Ah,' he said. 'I was of that guild too, but it was only honorary.'

'With Earth fallen, I wish to learn more of Earth in its pride.'

'Is all Earth fallen, then, and not only Roum?'

'I think it is so,' I said.

'Ah,' replied the Pilgrim. 'Ah!'

He fell silent and we went onward. I gave him my arm, and now he shuffled no longer, but moved with a young man's brisk stride. From time to time he uttered what might have been a sigh or a smothered sob. When I asked him details of his Pilgrimage, he answered obliquely or not at all. When we were an hour's journey outside Roum, and already amid forests, he said suddenly, 'This mask gives me pain. Will you help me adjust it?'

To my amazement he began to remove it. I gasped, for it is forbidden for a Pilgrim to reveal his face. Had he forgotten that I was not sightless too?

As the mask came away he said, 'You will not welcome this sight.'

The bronze grillwork slipped down from his forehead, and I saw first eyes that had been newly blinded, gaping holes where no surgeon's knife, but possibly thrusting fingers, had penetrated, and then the sharp regal nose, and finally the quirked, taut lips of the Prince of Roum.

'Your Majesty!' I cried.

Trails of dried blood ran down his cheeks. About the raw sockets themselves were smears of ointment. He felt little pain, I suppose, for he had killed it with those green smears, but the pain that burst through me was real and potent.

'Majesty no longer,' he said. 'Help me with the mask!' His hands trembled as he held it forth. 'These flanges must be widened. They press cruelly at my cheeks. Here — here—'

Quickly I made the adjustments, so that I would not have to see his ruined face for long.

He replaced the mask. 'I am a Pilgrim now,' he said quietly. 'Roum is without its Prince. Betray me if you

61

wish, Watcher; otherwise help me to Perris; and if ever I regain my power you will be well rewarded.'

'I am no betrayer,' I told him.

In silence we continued. I had no way of making small talk with such a man. It would be a somber journey for us to Perris; but I was committed now to be his guide. I thought of Gormon and how well he had kept his vows. I thought too of Avluela, and a hundred times the words leaped to my tongue to ask the fallen Prince how his consort the Flier had fared in the night of defeat, and I did not ask.

Twilight gathered, but the sun still gleamed golden-red before us in the west. And suddenly I halted and made a hoarse sound of surprise deep in my throat, as a shadow passed overhead.

High above me Avluela soared. Her skin was stained by the colors of the sunset, and her wings were spread to their fullest, radiant with every hue of the spectrum. She was already at least the height of a hundred men above the ground, and still climbing, and to her I must have been only a speck among the trees.

'What is it?' the Prince asked. 'What do you see?'

'Nothing.'

'Tell me what you see!'

I could not deceive him. 'I see a Flier, your Majesty. A slim girl far aloft.'

'Then the night must have come.'

'No,' I said. 'The sun is still above the horizon.'

'How can that be? She can only have nightwings. The sun would hurl her to the ground.'

I hesitated. I could not bring myself to explain how it was that Avluela flew by day, though she had only nightwings. I could not tell the Prince of Roum that beside her, wingless, flew the invader Gormon, effortlessly moving through the air, his arms about her thin shoulders, steadying her, supporting her, helping her resist the pressure of the solar wind. I could not tell him that his nemesis flew with the last of his consorts above his head.

'Well?' he demanded. 'How does she fly by day?'

'I do not know,' I said. 'It is a mystery to me. There are many things nowadays I can no longer understand.'

62

The Prince appeared to accept that. 'Yes, Watcher. Many things none of us can understand.'

He fell once more into silence. I yearned to call out to Avluela, but I knew she could not and would not hear me, and so I walked on toward the sunset, toward Perris, leading the blind Prince. And over us Avluela and Gormon sped onward, limned sharply against the day's last glow, until they climbed so high they were lost to my sight.

PART II

AMONG THE REMEMBERERS

1

To JOURNEY with a fallen Prince is no easy thing. His
eyes were gone, but not his pride; blinding had taught
him no humility. He wore the robes and mask of a Pilgrim,
but there was no piety in his soul and little grace. Behind
his mask he still knew himself to be the Prince of Roum.

I was all his court now, as we walked the road to Perris
in early springtime. I led him along the right roads; I
amused him at his command with stories of my wanderings;
I nursed him through moods of sulky bitterness. In return
I got very little except the assurance that I would eat regu-
larly. No one denies food to a Pilgrim, and in each village
on our way we stopped in inns, where he was fed and I,
as his companion, also was given meals. Once, early in our
travels, he erred and haughtily told an innkeeper, 'See that
you feed my servant as well!' The blinded Prince could not
see that look of shocked disbelief – for what would a Pilgrim be doing with a servant? – but I smiled at the innkeeper, and winked, and tapped my forehead, and the man
understood and served us both without discussion. Afterward I explained the error to the Prince, and thereafter he
spoke of me as his companion. Yet I knew that to him I was
nothing but a servant.

The weather was fair. Eyrop was growing warm as the
year turned. Slender willows and poplars were greening
beside the road, though much of the way out of Roum was
planted with lavish star-trees imported during the gaudy
days of the Second Cycle, and their blue-bladed leaves had
resisted our puny Eyropan winter. The birds, too, were
coming back from their season across the sea in Afreek.
They sparkled overhead, singing, discussing among themselves the change of masters in the world. 'They mock me,'

said the Prince one dawn. 'They sing to me and defy me to see their brightness!'

Oh, he was bitter, and with good reason. He, who had had so much and lost all, had a good deal to lament. For me, the defeat of Earth meant only an end to habits. Otherwise all was the same: no longer need I keep my Watch, but I still wandered the face of the world, alone even when, as now, I had a companion.

I wondered if the Prince knew why he had been blinded. I wondered if, in the moment of his triumph, Gormon had explained to the Prince that it was as elemental a matter as jealousy over a woman that had cost him his eyes.

'You took Avluela,' Gormon might have said. 'You saw a little Flier, and you thought she'd amuse you. And you said, here, girl, come to my bed. Not thinking of her as a person. Not thinking she might prefer others. Thinking only as a Prince of Roum might think – imperiously. Here, Prince!'

—and the quick, forked thrust of long-tipped fingers—

But I dared not ask. That much awe remained in me for this fallen monarch. To penetrate his privacy, to strike up a conversation with him about his mishaps as though he were an ordinary companion of the road – no, I could not. I spoke when I was spoken to. I offered conversation upon command. Otherwise I kept my silence, like a good commoner in the presence of royalty.

Each day we had our reminders that the Prince of Roum was royalty no longer.

Overhead flew the invaders, sometimes in floaters or other chariots, sometimes under their own power. Traffic was heavy. They were taking inventory of their world. Their shadows passed over us, tiny eclipses, and I looked up to see our new masters and oddly felt no anger at them, only relief that Earth's long vigil was over. For the Prince it was different. He always seemed to know when some invader passed above, and he clenched his fists, and scowled, and whispered black curses. Did his optic nerves still somehow record the movements of shadows? Or were his remaining senses so sharpened by the loss of one that he could detect the imperceptible humming of a floater and sniff the skins of the soaring invaders? I did not ask. I asked so little.

Sometimes at night, when he thought I slept, he sobbed. I pitied him then. He was so young to lose what he had, after all. I learned in those dark hours that even the sobs of a Prince are not those of ordinary men. He sobbed defiantly, belligerently, angrily. But yet he sobbed.

Much of the time he seemed stoic, resigned to his losses. He put one foot before the other and walked on briskly beside me, every step taking him farther from his great city of Roum, nearer to Perris. At other times, though, it seemed I could look through the bronze grillwork of his mask to see the curdled soul within. His pent-up rage took petty outlets. He mocked me for my age, for my low rank, for the emptiness of my life's purpose now that the invasion for which I had Watched had come. He toyed with me.

'Tell me your name, Watcher!'

'It is forbidden, Majesty.'

'Old laws are now repealed. Come on, man, we have months to travel together. Can I go on calling you Watcher all that time?'

'It is the custom of my guild.'

'The custom of mine,' he said, 'is to give orders and have them obeyed. Your name!'

'Not even the guild of Dominators can have a Watcher's name without due cause and a guildmaster's writ.'

He spat. 'What a jackal you are, to defy me when I'm like this! If we were in my palace now you'd never dare!'

'In your palace, Majesty, you would not make this unjust demand on me before your court. Dominators have obligations too. One of them is to respect the ways of lesser guilds.'

'He lectures me,' said the Prince. Irritably he threw himself down beside the road. Stretching against the grassy slope, he leaned back, touched one of the star-trees, snapped off a row of blades, clenched them in his hand so that they must have pricked his palm painfully. I stood beside him. A heavy land-vehicle rumbled by, the first we had seen on that empty road this morning. Within it were invaders. Some of them waved to us. After a long while the Prince said in a lighter, almost wheedling tone, 'My name is Enric. Now tell me yours.'

'I beg you to let me be, Majesty.'

'But you have my name! It is just as forbidden for me to give mine as you yours!'

'I did not ask yours,' I said firmly.

In the end I did not give him my name. It was a small enough victory, to refuse such information to a powerless Prince, but in a thousand little ways he made me pay for it. He nagged, chivvied, teased, cursed, and berated me. He spoke with contempt of my guild. He demanded menial services of me. I lubricated his metal mask; I sponged ointment into his ruined eyes; I did other things too humiliating to recall. And so we stumbled along the highway to Perris, the empty old man and the emptied young man, full of hatred for one another, and yet bound by the needs and the duties of wayfarers.

It was a difficult time. I had to cope with his changing moods as he soared to cosmic rapture over his plans for redeeming conquered Earth, and as he sank to abysses upon his realization that the conquest was final. I had to protect him from his own rashness in the villages, where he sometimes behaved as though he were still Prince of Roum, ordering folk about, slapping them even, in a way that was unbecoming to a holy man. Worse yet, I had to minister to his lusts, buying him women who came to him in darkness, unaware that they were dealing with one who claimed to be a Pilgrim. As a Pilgrim he was a fraud, for he did not carry the starstone with which Pilgrims make communion with the Will. Somehow I got him past all of these crises, even the time when we encountered on the road another Pilgrim, a genuine one. This was a formidable and disputatious old man full of theological quibbles. 'Come and talk with me of the immanence of the Will,' he said to the Prince, and the Prince, whose patience was frayed that afternoon, replied obscenely. I kicked the princely shin in a surreptitious way, and to the shocked Pilgrim I said, 'Our friend is unwell today. Last night he held communion with the Will and received a revelation that unsettled his mind. I pray you, let us go on, and give him no talk of holiness until he is himself once more.'

With such improvisations I managed our journey.

As the weather warmed, the Prince's attitude mellowed. Perhaps he was growing reconciled to his catastrophe, or possibly, in the prison of his lightless skull, he was teaching himself new tactics for meeting his changed existence. He talked almost idly of himself, his downfall, his humiliation. He spoke of the power that had been his in terms that said unmistakably that he had no illusions about ever recapturing it. He talked of his wealth, his women, his jewels, his strange machines, his Changelings and Musicians and Servitors, the Masters and even fellow Dominators who had knelt to him. I will not say that at any time I liked him, but at least at these times I recognized a suffering human being behind his impassive mask.

He even recognized in me a human being. I know it cost him much.

He said, 'The trouble with power, Watcher, is that it cuts you off from people. People become things. Take yourself. To me, you were nothing but a machine that walked around Watching for invaders. I suppose you had dreams, ambitions, angers, all the rest, but I saw you as a dried-up old man without any independent existence outside of your guild function. Now I see much more by seeing nothing.'

'What do you see?'

'You were young once, Watcher. You had a town you loved. A family. A girl, even. You chose, or had chosen for you, a guild, you went into apprenticeship, you struggled, your head ached you, your belly griped you, there were many dark moments when you wondered what it was all about, what it was for. And you saw us ride by, Masters, Dominators, and it was like comets going past. Yet here we are together, cast up by the tides on the road to Perris. And which of us is happier now?'

'I am beyond happiness or sorrow,' I said.

'Is that the truth? Is that the truth? Or is it a line you hide behind? Tell me, Watcher: I know your guild forbids you to marry, but have you ever loved?'

'Sometimes.'

'And are you beyond that now?'

'I am old,' I said evasively.

'But you could love. You could love. You're released from your guild vows now, eh? You could take a bride.'

I laughed. 'Who'd have me?'

'Don't speak that way. You're not that old. You have strengths. You've seen the world, you understand it. Why, in Perris you could find yourself some wench who—' He paused. 'Were you ever tempted, while you still were under your vows?'

Just then a Flier passed overhead. She was a woman of middle years, struggling a little in the sky, for some daylight remained to press on her wings. I felt a pang, and I wanted to tell the Prince: yes, yes, I was tempted, there was a little Flier not long ago, a girl, a child, Avluela; and in my way I loved her, though I never touched her; and I love her still.

I said nothing to Prince Enric.

I looked, though, at that Flier, freer than I because she had wings, and in the warmth of that spring evening I felt the chill of desolation enfolding me.

'Is it far to Perris?' the Prince asked.

'We will walk, and one day we will get there.'

'And then?'

'For me an apprenticeship in the guild of Rememberers, and a new life. For you?'

'I hope to find friends there,' he said.

We walked on, long hours each day. There were those who went by and offered us rides, but we refused, for at the checkpoints the invaders would be seeking such wandering nobility as the Prince. We walked a tunnel miles long under sky-storming mountains sheathed in ice, and we entered a flat land of farming peasants, and we paused by awakening rivers to cool our toes. Golden summer burst upon us. We moved through the world but were not of it; we listened to no news of the conquest, although it was obvious that the invaders had taken full possession. In small vehicles they hovered everywhere, seeing our world that now was theirs.

I did the bidding of the Prince in all ways, including the unpleasant ones. I attempted to make his life less bleak. I gave him a sensation of being still a ruler – albeit of only one useless old Watcher. I taught him, too, how best to masquerade as a Pilgrim. From what little I knew I gave him postures, phrases, prayers. It was obvious that he had spent little time in contact with the Will while he reigned. Now he pretended faith, but it was insincere, part of his camouflage.

In a town called Dijon, he said, 'Here I will purchase eyes.'

Not true eyes. The secret of making such replacements perished in the Second Cycle. Out among the more fortunate stars any miracle is available for a price, but our Earth is a neglected world in a backwater of the universe. The Prince might have got out there in the days before conquest to purchase new sight, but now the best that was available to him was a way of distinguishing light from dark. Even that would give him a rudiment of sight; at present he had no other guidance than the reverberator that warned him of obstacles in his path. How did he know, though, that in Dijon he would find a craftsman with the necessary skills? And with what would he meet the cost?

He said, 'The man here is a brother of one of my Scribes. He is of the guild of Artificers, and I often bought his work in Roum. He'll have eyes for me.'

'And the cost?'

'I am not entirely without resources.'

We stopped in a field of gnarled cork-trees, and the Prince undid his robes. Indicating a place in the fleshy part of his thigh, he said, 'I carry a reserve here for emergencies. Give me your blade!' I handed it to him, and he seized the handle and pressed the stud that brought forth the cool, keen beam of light. With his left hand he felt his thigh, surveying for the exact place; then, stretching the flesh between two fingers, he made a surgically precise cut two inches long. He did not bleed, nor was there a sign that he felt pain. I watched in bewilderment as he slipped his fingers into the cut, spread its edges, and seemed to grope as if in a sack. He tossed my blade back to me.

Treasures tumbled from his thigh.

'Watch that nothing is lost,' he ordered me.

To the grass there fell seven sparkling jewels of alien origin, a small and artful celestial globe, five golden coins of Imperial Roum of cycles past, a ring set with a glowing dab of quasi-life, a flask of some unknown perfume, a group of miniature musical instruments done in precious woods and metals, eight statuettes of regal-looking men, and more. I scooped these wonders into a dazzling heap.

'An overpocket,' the Prince said coolly, 'which a skilled Surgeon implanted in my flesh. I anticipated a time of crisis in which I might need to leave the palace hurriedly. Into it I stuffed what I could; there is much more where these came from. Tell me, tell me what I have taken out!'

I gave him the full inventory. He listened tensely to the end, and I knew that he had kept count of all that had poured forth, and was testing my honesty. When I was done, he nodded, pleased. 'Take the globe,' he said, 'and the ring, and the two brightest jewels. Hide them in your pouch. The rest goes back within.' He spread the lips of the incision, and one by one I dropped the glories inside, where they joined who knew what splendid things lying in another dimension, the outlet from which was embedded in the Prince. He might have half the contents of the palace tucked away in his thigh. At the end he pressed the cut together, and it healed without a trace of a mark as I watched. He robed himself.

In town we quickly located the shop of Bordo the Artificer. He was a squat man with a speckled face, a grizzled beard, a tic in one eye, and a flat coarse nose, but his fingers were as delicate as a woman's. His shop was a dark place with dusty wooden shelves and small windows; It could have been a building ten thousand years old. A few elegant items were on display. Most were not. He looked at us guardedly, obviously baffled that a Watcher and a Pilgrim should come to him.

At the Prince's prodding I said, 'My friend needs eyes.'

'I make a devise, yes. But it is expensive, and it takes many months to prepare. Beyond the means of any Pilgrim.' I laid one jewel on the weathered counter. 'We have means.'

Shaken, Bordo snatched up the jewel, turned it this way and that, saw alien fires glowing at its heart.

'If you come back when the leaves are falling—'

'You have no eyes in stock?' I asked.

He smiled. 'I get few calls for such things. We keep a small inventory.'

I put down the celestial globe. Bordo recognized it as the work of a master, and his jaw sagged. He put it in one palm and tugged at his beard with the other hand. I let him look at it long enough to fall in love with it, and then I took it back and said, 'Autumn is too long to wait. We will have to go elsewhere. Perris, perhaps.' I caught the Prince's elbow, and we shuffled toward the door.

'Stop!' Bordo cried. 'At least let me check! Perhaps I have a pair somewhere—' And he began to rummage furiously in overpockets mounted in the rear wall.

He had eyes in stock, of course, and I haggled a bit on the price, and we settled for the globe, the ring, and one jewel. The Prince was silent throughout the transaction. I insisted on immediate installation and Bordo, nodding excitedly, shut his shop, slipped on a thinking cap, and summoned a sallow-faced Surgeon. Shortly the preliminaries of the operation were under way. The Prince lay on a pallet in a sealed and sterile room. He removed his reverberator and then his mask; and as those sharp features came into view, Bordo – who had been to the court of Roum – grunted in amazement and began to say something. My foot descended heavily on his. Bordo swallowed his words; and the Surgeon, unaware, began tranquilly to swab the ruined sockets.

The eyes were pearl-gray spheres, smaller than real eyes and broken by transverse slits. What mechanism was within I do not know, but from their rear projected tiny golden connections to fasten to the nerves. The Prince slept through the early part of the task, while I stood guard and Bordo assisted the Surgeon. Then it was necessary to awaken him. His face convulsed in pain, but it was so quickly mastered that Bordo muttered a prayer at this display of determination.

'Some light here,' said the Surgeon.

Bordo nudged a drifting globe closer. The Prince said, 'Yes, yes, I see the difference.'

'We must test. We must adjust,' the Surgeon said.

Bordo went outside. I followed. The man was trembling, and his face was green with fear.

'Will you kill us now?' he asked.

'Of course not.'

'I recognized—'

'You recognized a poor Pilgrim,' I said, 'who has suffered a terrible misfortune while on his journey. No more. Nothing else.'

I examined Bordo's stock awhile. Then the Surgeon and his patient emerged. The Prince now bore the pearly spheres in his sockets, with a meniscus of false flesh about them to insure a tight fit. He looked more machine than man, with those dead things beneath his brows, and as he moved his head the slits widened, narrowed, widened again, silently, stealthily. 'Look,' he said, and walked across the room, indicating objects, even naming them. I knew that he saw as though through a thick veil, but at least he saw, in a fashion. He masked himself again and by nightfall we were gone from Dijon.

The Prince seemed almost buoyant. But what he had in his skull was a poor substitute for what Gormon had ripped from him, and soon enough he knew it. That night, as we slept on stale cots in a Pilgrim's hostelry, the Prince cried out in wordless sounds of fury, and by the shifting light of the true moon and the two false ones I saw his arms rise, his fingers curl, his nails strike at an imagined enemy, and strike again, and again.

2

IT WAS summer's end when we finally reached Perris.
We came into the city from the south, walking a broad,
resilient highway bordered by ancient trees, amid a fine
shower of rain. Gusts of wind blew shriveled leaves about
us. That night of terror on which we both had fled conquered Roum now seemed almost a dream; we were
toughened by a spring and summer of walking, and the gray
towers of Perris seemed to hold out promise of new begin-
nings. I suspected that we deceived ourselves, for what did
the world hold for a shattered Prince who saw only shadows,
and a Watcher long past his proper years?

This was a darker city than Roum. Even in late winter,
Roum had had clear skies and bright sunlight. Perris
seemed perpetually clouded over, buildings and environment
both somber. Even the city walls were ash-gray, and they
had no sheen. The gate stood wide. Beside it there lounged
a small, sullen man in the garb of the guild of Sentinels,
who made no move to challenge us as we approached. I
looked at him questioningly. He shook his head.

'Go in, Watcher.'

'Without a check?'

'You haven't heard? All cities were declared free six
nights ago. Order of the invaders. Gates are never closed
now. Half the Sentinels have no work.'

'I thought the invaders were searching for enemies,' I
said. 'The former nobility.'

'They have their checkpoints elsewhere, and no Sentinels
are used. The city is free. Go in. Go in.'

As we went in, I said, 'Then why are you here?'

'It was my post for forty years,' the Sentinel said. 'Where
should I go?'

I made the sign that told him I shared his sorrow, and
the Prince and I entered Perris.

'Five times I came to Perris by the southern gate,' said
the Prince. 'Always by chariot, with my Changelings walking

before me and making music in their throats. We proceeded to the river, past the ancient buildings and monuments, on to the palace of the Comt of Perris. And by night we danced on gravity plates high above the city, and there were ballets of Fliers, and from the Tower of Perris there was performed an aurora for us. And the wine, the red wine of Perris, the women in their saucy gowns, the red-tipped breasts, the sweet thighs! We bathed in wine, Watcher.' He pointed vaguely. 'Is that the Tower of Perris?'

'I think it is the ruin of this city's weather machine,' I said.

'A weather machine would be a vertical column. What I see rises from a wide base to a slender summit, as does the Tower of Perris.'

'What I see,' I said gently, 'is a vertical column, at least thirty men high, ending in a rough break. The Tower would not be this close to the southern gate, would it?'

'No,' said the Prince, and muttered a foulness. 'The weather machine it is, then. These eyes of Bordo's don't see so clearly for me, eh? I deceive myself, Watcher. I deceive myself. Find a thinking cap and see if the Comt has fled.'

I stared a moment longer at the truncated pillar of the weather machine, that fantastic device which had brought such grief upon the world in the Second Cycle. I tried to penetrate its sleek, almost oily marble sides, to see the coiling intestines of mysterious devices that had been capable of sinking whole continents, that long ago had transformed my homeland in the west from a mountainous country to a chain of islands. Then I turned away, donned a public cap, asked for the Comt, got the answer I expected, and demanded to know the locations of places where we might find lodging.

The Prince said, 'Well?'

'The Comt of Perris was slain during the conquest along with all his sons. His dynasty is extinguished, his title is abolished, his palace has been transformed into a museum by the invaders. The rest of the Perrisian nobility is dead or has taken flight. I'll find a place for you at the lodge of Pilgrims.'

'No. Take me with you to the Rememberers.'

'Is that the guild you seek now?'

He gestured impatiently. 'No, fool! But how can I stay alone in a strange city, with all my friends gone? What would I say to true Pilgrims in their hostelry? I'll stay with you. The Rememberers can hardly turn away a blind Pilgrim.'

He gave me no choice. And so he accompanied me to the Hall of Rememberers.

We had to cross half the city, and it took us nearly the whole day. Perris seemed to me to be in disarray. The coming of the invaders had upset the structure of our society, liberating from their tasks great blocs of people, in some cases whole guilds. I saw dozens of my fellow Watchers in the streets, some still dragging about with them their cases of instruments, others, like me, freed of that burden and scarcely knowing what to do with their hands. My guildmates looked glum and hollow; many of them were dull-eyed with carousing, now that all discipline was shattered. Then there were Sentinels, aimless and dispirited because they had nothing to guard, and Defenders, cowed and dazed at the ending of defense. I saw no Masters and of course no Dominators, but many unemployed Clowns, Musicians, Scribes, and other court functionaries drifted randomly. Also there were hordes of dull neuters, their nearly mindless bodies slumped from unfamiliar disuse. Only Vendors and Somnambulists seemed to be carrying on business as usual.

The invaders were very much in evidence. In twos and threes they strolled on every street, long-limbed beings whose hands dangled nearly to their knees; their eyelids were heavy, their nostrils were hidden in filtration pouches, their lips were full and, when not apart, joined almost seamlessly. Most of them were dressed in identical robes of a deep, rich green, perhaps a uniform of military occupation; a few carried weapons of an oddly primitive kind, great heavy things slung across their backs, probably more for display than for self-defense. They seemed generally relaxed as they moved among us – genial conquerors, self-confident and proud, fearing no molestation from the defeated populace. Yet the fact that they never walked alone argued that they felt an inner wariness. I could not find it in me to resent their presence, nor even the implied arrogance of their possessive glances at the ancient monuments of Perris; yet the Prince of Roum, to whom all figures were merely upright bars of dark gray against a field of light gray, instinctively sensed their nearness to him and reacted with quick hostile intakes of breath.

Also there were many more outworld visitors than usual, star-beings of a hundred kinds, some able to breathe our air, others going about in hermetic globes or little pyramid-shaped breathing-boxes or contour suits. It was nothing new to see such strangers on Earth, of course, but the sheer quantity of them was astonishing. They were everywhere, prowling into the houses of Earth's old religion, buying shining models of the Tower of Perris from Vendors at street corners, clambering precariously into the upper levels of the walkways, peering into occupied dwellings, snapping images, exchanging currency with furtive hucksters, flirting with Fliers and Somnambulists, risking their lives at our restaurants, moving in shepherded groups from sight to sight. It was as though our invaders had passed the word through the galaxies: SEE OLD EARTH NOW. UNDER NEW MANAGEMENT.

At least our beggars were flourishing. The outworld ones fared poorly at the hands of the alien almsgivers, but those who were Earthborn did well, except for the Changelings, who could not be recognized as native stock. I saw several of these mutants, disgruntled at being refused, turn on other beggars who had had better luck and beat them to the ground, while image-snappers recorded the scene for the delight of galactic stay-at-homes.

We came in time to the Hall of Rememberers.

It was an imposing building, as well it might be, housing as it did all our planet's past. It rose to an enormous height on the southern bank of the Senn, just opposite the equally massive palace of the Comt. But the dwelling of the deposed Comt was an ancient building, truly ancient, of the First Cycle even, a long, involuted structure of gray stone with a green metal roof in the traditional Perrisian style, while the Hall of Rememberers was a shaft of polished whiteness, its surface unbroken by windows, about which there coiled from summit to base a golden helix of burnished metal that bore inscribed on it the history of mankind. The upper coils of the helix were blank. At a distance I could read nothing, and I wondered whether the Rememberers had taken the trouble to inscribe upon their building the tale of Earth's final defeat. Later I learned that they had not – that the story, in fact, terminated at the end of the Second Cycle, leaving untold much for which little pleasure was felt.

Night was falling now. And Perris, which had looked so dreary in the clouded and drizzly day, came to beauty like a dowager returning from Jorslem with her youth and voluptuousness restored. The city's lights cast a soft but dazzling radiance that magically illuminated the old gray buildings, turning angles hazy, hiding antiquity's grime, blurring ugliness into poetry. The Comt's palace was transformed from a heavy thing of sprawling bulk into an airy fable. The Tower of Perris, spotlighted against the dusk, loomed above us to the east like a giant gaunt spider, but a spider of grace and charm. The whiteness of the Hall of Rememberers was now intolerably beautiful, and the helical coil of history no longer seemed to wind to the summit, but plunged directly into one's heart. The Fliers of Perris were abroad at this hour, taking their ease above us in a graceful ballet, their filmy wings spread wide to catch the light from below, their slender bodies trailing at an angle to the horizon. How they soared, these genetically altered children of Earth, these fortunate members of a guild that demands only that its members find pleasure in life! They shed beauty upon the groundlings like little moons. They were joined in their airborne dance by invaders, flying in some method unknown to me, their lengthy limbs drawn close to their bodies. I noticed that the Fliers showed no distaste for those who had come to share their sport, but rather appeared to welcome the outworlders, allowing them places in the dance.

Higher, on the backdrop of the sky itself, whirled the two false moons, blank and burnished, skimming from west to east; and blobs of disciplined light swirled in midatmosphere in what I supposed was a customary Perisian diversion; and speakers floating beneath the clouds showered us with sparkling music. I heard the laughter of girls from somewhere; I scented bubbling wine. If this is Perris conquered, I wondered, what must Perris free have been like?

79

'Are we at the Hall of Rememberers?' asked Prince Enric testily.

'This is it, yes,' I replied. 'A tower of white.'

'I know what it looks like, idiot! But now – I see less well after dark – that building there?'

'You point to the palace of the Comt, Majesty.'

'There, then.'

'Yes.'

'Why have we not gone in?'

'I am seeing Perris,' I said. 'I have never known such beauty. Roum is attractive too, in a different way. Roum is an emperor; Perris is a courtesan.'

'You talk poetry, you shriveled old man!'

'I feel my age dropping away. I could dance in the streets now. This city sings to me.'

'Go in. Go in. We are here to see the Rememberers. Let it sing to you later.'

I sighed and guided him toward the entrance to the great hall. We passed up a walkway of some black glossy stone, while beams of light played down on us, scanning us and recording us. A monstrous ebon door, five men wide and ten men high, proved to be only a projected illusion, for as we neared it I sensed the depth of it, saw its vaulted interior, and knew it for a deception. I felt a vague warmth and tasted a strange perfume as we passed through it.

Within was a mammoth antechamber nearly as awesome as the grand inner space of the palace of the Prince of Roum. All was white, the stone glowing with an inner radiance that bathed everything in brilliance. To right and left, heavy doorways led to inner wings. Although night had come, many individuals were clustered about access banks mounted on the rear wall of the antechamber, where screens and caps gave them contact with the massive files of the guild of Rememberers. I noticed with interest that many of those who had come here with questions about mankind's past were invaders.

Our footsteps crackled on the tiled floor as we crossed it.

I saw no actual Rememberers, and so I went to an access bank, put on a thinking cap, and notified the embalmed brain to which it was connected that I sought the Rememberer Basil, he whom I had met briefly in Roum.

'What is your business with him?'

'I bring with me his shawl, which he left in my care when he fled Roum.'

'The Rememberer Basil has returned to Roum to complete his research, by permission of the conqueror. I will send to you another member of the guild to receive the shawl.'

We did not have long to wait. We stood together near the rear of the antechamber, and I contemplated the spectacle of the invaders who had so much to learn, and in moments there came to us a thick-set, dour-faced man some years younger than myself, but yet not young, who wore about his broad shoulders the ceremonial shawl of his guild.

'I am the Rememberer Elegro,' he announced portentously.

'I bring you Basil's shawl.'

'Come. Follow.'

He had emerged from an imperceptible place in the wall where a sliding block turned on pivots. Now he slid it once more and rapidly went down a passageway. I called out to him that my companion was blind and could not match his pace, and the Rememberer Elegro halted, looking visibly impatient. His downcurving mouth twitched, and he buried his short fingers in the deep black curls of his beard. When we had caught up with him he moved on less swiftly. We pursued an infinity of passageways and ended in Elegro's domicile, somewhere high in the tower.

The room was dark but amply furnished with screens, caps, scribing equipment, voice-boxes, and other aids to scholarship. The walls were hung with a purple-black fabric, evidently alive, for its marginal folds rippled in pulsating rhythms. Three drifting globes gave less than ample light.

'The shawl,' he said.

I produced it from my pouch. It had amused me to wear it for a while in those first confused days of the conquest – after all, Basil had left it in my hands when he fled down the street, and I had not meant to wrest it from him, but he obviously had cared little for its loss – but shortly I had put it away, since it bred confusion for a man in Watcher's garb to wear a Rememberer's shawl. Elegro took it from me curtly and unfolded it, scrutinizing it as though looking for lice.

'How did you get this?'

'Basil and I encountered one another in the street during the actual moment of the invasion. He was highly agitated. I attempted to restrain him and he ran past me, leaving me still grasping his shawl.'

'He told a different story.'

'I regret if I have compromised him,' I said.

'At any rate, you have returned his shawl. I'll communicate the news to Roum tonight. Are you expecting a reward for delivering it?'

'Yes.'

Displeased, Elegro said, 'Which is?'

'To be allowed to come among the Rememberers as an apprentice.'

He looked startled. 'You have a guild!'

'To be a Watcher in these days is to be guildless. For what should I watch? I am released from my vows.'

'Perhaps. But you are old to be trying a new guild.'

'Not *too* old.'

'Ours is a difficult one.'

'I am willing to work hard. I desire to learn. In my old age curiosity is born in me.'

'Become a Pilgrim like your friend here. See the world.'

'I have seen the world. Now I wish to join the Rememberers and learn of the past.'

'You can dial an information below. Our access banks are open to you, Watcher.'

'It is not the same. Enroll me.'

'Apprentice yourself to the Indexers,' Elegro suggested. 'The work is similar, but not so demanding.'

'I claim apprenticeship here.'

Elegro sighed heavily. He steepled his fingers, bowed his head, quirked his lips. This was plainly unique to him. While he pondered, an inner door opened and a female Rememberer entered the room, carrying a small turquoise music-sphere cradled in both her hands. She took four paces and halted, obviously surprised that Elegro was entertaining visitors.

She made a nod of apology and said, 'I will return later.'

'Stay,' said the Rememberer. To myself and the Prince he said, 'My wife. The Rememberer Olmayne.' To his wife he said, 'These are travelers newly come from Roum. They

82

have delivered Basil's shawl. The Watcher now asks apprenticeship in our guild. What do you advise?'

The Rememberer Olmayne's white brow furrowed. She put down her music-sphere in a dark crystal vase; the sphere was unintentionally activated as she did so, and it offered us a dozen shimmering notes before she switched it off. Then she contemplated us, and I her. She was notably younger than her husband, who was of middle years, while she seemed to be hardly past first bloom. Yet there was a strength about her that argued for greater maturity. Perhaps, I thought, she had been to Jorslem to renew her youth; but in that case it was odd that her husband had not done the same, unless he prized his look of age. She was surely attractive. Her face was broad, with a high forehead, pronounced cheekbones, a wide, sensual mouth, a jutting chin. Her hair was lustrous black, constrasting most vividly with the pallor of her skin. Such white skin is a rarity among us, though now I know that it was more common in ancient times, when the breed was different. Avluela, my lovely little Flier, had displayed that same combination of black and white, but there the resemblance ended, for Avluela was all fragility, and the Rememberer Olmayne was strength itself. Below her long slender neck her body blossomed into well-set shoulders, high breasts, firm legs. Her posture was regal.

She studied us at length, until I could scarcely meet the level gaze of her widely spaced dark eyes. Ultimately she said, 'Does the Watcher regard himself as qualified to become one of us?'

The question appeared aimed at anyone in the chamber who cared to reply. I hesitated; Elegro did likewise; and at length it was the Prince of Roum who replied in his voice of command, 'The Watcher is qualified to enter your guild.'

'And who are you?' Olmayne demanded.

Instantly the Prince adopted a more accommodating tone. 'A miserable blind Pilgrim, milady, who has wandered here on foot from Roum, in this man's company. If I am any judge, you could do worse than admit him as an apprentice.'

Elegro said, 'And yourself? What plans have you?'

'I wish only refuge here,' said the Prince. 'I am tired of roaming and there is much thinking I must do. Perhaps you could allow me to carry out small tasks here. I would not want to be separated from my companion.'

To me Olmayne said, 'We will confer on your case. If there is approval, you will be given the tests. I will be your sponsor.'

'Olmayne!' blurted Elegro in unmistakable amazement.

She smiled serenely at us all.

A family quarrel appeared on the verge; but it was averted, and the Rememberers offered us hospitality, juices, sharper beverages, a night's lodging. We dined apart from them in one section of their suite, while other Rememberers were summoned to consider my irregular application. The Prince seemed in strange agitation; he bolted down his food, spilled a flask of wine, fumbled with his eating utensils, put his fingers again and again to his gray metallic eyeballs as though trying to scratch an itch upon the lobes of his brain.

At length he said in a low, urgent voice, 'Describe her to me!'

I did so, in detail, coloring and shading my words to draw him the most vivid pictures I could.

'She is beautiful, you say?'

'I believe so. You know that at my age one must work from abstract notions, not from the flow of the glands.'

'Her voice arouses me,' said the Prince. 'She has power. She is queenly. She *must* be beautiful; there'd be no justice if her body failed to match the voice.'

'She is,' I said heavily, 'another man's wife, and the giver of hospitality.'

I remembered a day in Roum when the Prince's palanquin had come forth from the palace, and the Prince had spied Avluela, and ordered her to him, drawing her through the curtain to make use of her. A Dominator may command lesser folk that way; but a Pilgrim may not, and I feared Prince Enric's schemes now. He dabbed at his eyes again. His facial muscles worked.

'Promise me you'll not start trouble with her,' I said.

The corner of his mouth jerked in what must have been the beginning of an angry retort, quickly stifled. With effort he said, 'You misjudge me, old man. I'll abide by the laws of hospitality here. Be a good man and get me more wine, eh?'

I thumbed the serving niche and obtained a second flask.

It was strong red wine, not the golden stuff of Roum. I poured; we drank; the flask was swiftly empty. I grasped it along its lines of polarity and gave it the proper twist, and it popped and was gone like a bubble. Moments later the Rememberer Olmayne entered. She had changed her garments; earlier she had worn an afternoon gown of dull hue and coarse fabric, but now she was garbed in a sheer scarlet robe fastened between her breasts. It revealed to me the planes and shadows of her body, and it surprised me to see that she had chosen to retain a navel. It broke the smooth downward sweep of her belly in an effect so carefully calculated to arouse that it nearly incited even me.

She said complacently, 'Your application has been approved under my sponsorship. The tests will be administered tonight. If you succeed, you will be pledged to our division.' Her eyes twinkled in sudden mischief. 'My husband, you should know, is most displeased. But my husband's displeasure is not a thing to be feared. Come with me, both of you.'

She stretched forth her hands, taking mine, taking the Prince's. Her fingers were cool. I throbbed with an inner fever and marveled at this sign of new youth that arose within me – not even by virtue of the waters of the house of renewal in sacred Jorslem.

'Come,' said Olmayne, and led us to the place of test.

85

3

AND so I passed into the guild of Rememberers.

The tests were perfunctory. Olmayne brought us to a circular room somewhere near the summit of the great tower. Its curving walls were inlaid with rare woods of many hues, and shining benches rose from the floor, and in the center of all was a helix the height of a man, inscribed with letters too small to be read. Half a dozen Rememberers lounged about, plainly there only by Olmayne's whim, and not in the slightest interested in this old and shabby Watcher whom she had so unaccountably sponsored.

A thinking cap was offered me. A scratchy voice asked me a dozen questions through the cap, probing for my typical responses, querying me on biographical details. I gave my guild identification so that they could contact the local guildmaster, check my *bona fides,* and obtain my release. Ordinarily one could not win release from a Watcher's vows, but these were not ordinary times, and I knew my guild was shattered.

Within an hour all was done. Olmayne herself placed the shawl over my shoulders.

'You'll be given sleeping quarters near our suite,' she said. 'You'll have to surrender your Watcher garb, though your friend may remain in Pilgrim's clothes. Your training will begin after a probationary period. Meanwhile you have full access to any of our memory tanks. You realize, of course, that it will be ten years or more before you can win full admission to the guild.'

'I realize that,' I said.

'Your name now will be Tomis,' Olmayne told me. 'Not yet the Rememberer Tomis, but Tomis of the Rememberers. There is a difference. Your past name no longer matters.'

The Prince and I were conducted to the small room we would share. It was a humble enough place, but yet it had facilities for washing, outlets for thinking caps and other information devices, and a food vent. Prince Enric went about the room, touching things, learning the geography. Cabinets, beds, chairs, storage units, and other furniture popped in and out of the walls as he blundered onto the controls. Eventually he was satisfied; not blundering now, he activated a bed, and a sheaf of brightness glided from a slot. He stretched out.

'Tell me something, Tomis of the Rememberers.'

'Yes?'

'To satisfy curiosity that eats me. What was your name in previous life?'

'It does not matter now.'

'No vows bind you to secrecy. Will you thwart me still?'

'Old habit binds me,' I said. 'For twice your lifetime I was conditioned never to speak my name except lawfully.'

'Speak it now.'

'Wuellig,' I said.

It was strangely liberating to commit that act. My former name seemed to hover in the air before my lips; to dart from the room like a jewelbird released from its captivity; to soar, to turn sharply, to strike a wall and shiver to pieces with a light, tinkling sound. I trembled, 'Wuellig,' I said again. 'My name was Wuellig.'

'Wuellig no more.'

'Tomis of the Rememberers.'

And we both laughed until it hurt, and the blinded Prince swung himself to his feet and slapped his hand against mine in high good fellowship, and we shouted my name and his and mine again and again, like small boys who suddenly have learned the words of power and have discovered at last how little power those words really have.

Thus I took up my new life among the Rememberers.

For some time to come I did not leave the Hall of Rememberers at all. My days and nights were completely occupied, and I remained a stranger to Perris without. The Prince, too, though his time was not as fully taken up, stayed in the building almost always, going out only when boredom or fury overtook him. Occasionally the Rememberer Olmayne went with him, or he with her, so that he would not be alone in his darkness; but I know that on occasion he left the building by himself, defiantly intending to show that, even sightless, he could cope with the challenges of the city.

My waking hours were divided among these activities:

+ Primary orientations.
+ Menial duties of an apprentice.
+ Private researches.

Not unexpectedly, I found myself much older than the other apprentices then in residence. Most were youngsters, the children of Rememberers themselves; they looked upon me in bafflement, unable to comprehend having such an ancient for a schoolmate. There were a few fairly mature apprentices, those who had found a vocation for Remembering midway in life, but none approaching my age. Hence I had little social contact with my fellows in training.

For a part of each day we learned the techniques by which the Rememberers recapture Earth's past. I was shown wide-eyed through the laboratories where analysis of field specimens is performed; I saw the detectors which, by pinpointing the decay of a few atoms, give an age to an artifact; I watched as beams of many-colored light lancing from a ringed outlet turned a sliver of wood to ash and caused it to give up its secrets; I saw the very images of past events peeled from inanimate substance. We leave our imprint where we go: the particles of light rebound from our faces, and the photonic flux nails them to the environment. From which the Rememberers strip them, categorize them, fix them. I entered a room where a phantasmagoria of faces drifted on a greasy blue mist: vanished kings and guildmasters, lost dukes, heroes of ancient days. I beheld cold-eyed technicians prodding history from handfuls of charred matter. I saw damp lumps of trash give up tales of revolutions and assassinations, of cultural change, of the discarding of mores.

Then I was instructed superficially in the techniques of the field. Through cunning simulation I was shown Rememberers at work with vacuum cores digging through the mounds of the great ruined cities of Afreek and Ais. I participated vicariously in the undersea quest for the remnants of the civilizations of the Lost Continents; teams of Rememberers entered translucent, teardrop-shaped vehicles like blobs of green gelatin and sped into the depths of Earth Ocean, down and down to the slime-crusted prairies

of the former land and with dancing beams of violet force,
they drilled through muck and girders to find buried truths.
I watched the gatherers of shards, the diggers of shadows,
the collectors of molecular films. One of the best of the
orientation experiences they provided was a sequence in
which truly heroic Rememberers excavated a weather machine in lower Afreek, baring the base of the titanic thing,
lifting it on power pulls from the soil, an extraction so
mighty that the earth itself seemed to shriek when it was
done. High aloft they floated the ponderous relic of Second
Cycle folly, while shawled experts prodded in its root-place
to learn how the column had been erected in the first in-
stance. My eyes throbbed at the spectacle.

I emerged from the sessions with an overwhelming awe
for this guild I had chosen. Individual Rememberers whom
I had known had struck me generally as pompous, disdainful, haughty, or merely aloof; I did not find them charming.
Yet is the whole greater than the sum of its parts, and I
saw such men as Basil and Elegro, so vacant, so absent from
ordinary human concerns, so disinterested, as part of a colossal effort to win back from eternity our brilliant yesterdays. This research into lost time was magnificent, the only
proper substitute for mankind's former activities; having
lost our present and our future, we had of necessity to bend
all our endeavors to the past, which no one could take from
us if only we were vigilant enough.

For many days I absorbed the details of this effort, every
stage of the work from the collection of specks of dust in
the field through their treatment and analysis in the laboratory to the highest endeavor of all, synthesis and interpre-
tation, which was carried out by senior Rememberers on the
highest level of this building. I was given but a glimpse of
those sages: withered and dry, old enough to be grand-
fathers to me, white heads bent forward, thin lips droning
comments and interpretations, quibbles and corrections.
Some of them, I was told in a hushed whisper, had been
renewed at Jorslem two and three times apiece, and now
were beyond renewal and in their final great age.

Next we were introduced to the memory tanks where the
Rememberers store their findings, and from which are dis-
pensed informations for the benefit of the curious.

As a Watcher I had had little curiosity and less interest in visiting memory tanks. Certainly I had never seen anything like this, for the tanks of the Rememberers were no mere three-brain or five-brain storage units, but mammoth installations with a hundred brains or more hooked in series. The room to which they took us – one of dozens beneath the building, I learned – was an oblong chamber, deep but not high, in which brain cases were arrayed in rows of nine that faded into shadowed depths. Perspective played odd tricks; I was not sure if there were ten rows or fifty, and the sight of those bleached domes was overpoweringly immense.

'Are these the brains of former Rememberers?' I asked.

The guide replied, 'Some of them are. But there's no necessity to use only Rememberers. Any normal human brain will do; even a Servitor has more storage capacity than you'd believe. We have no need for redundancy in our circuits, and so we can use the full resources of each brain.'

I tried to peer through the heavy block of sleekness that protected the memory tanks from harm. I said, 'What is recorded in this particular room?'

'The names of dwellers in Afreek in Second Cycle times, and as much personal data about each as we have so far recovered. Also, since these cells are not fully charged, we have temporarily stored in them certain geographical details concerning the Lost Continents, and information pertaining to the creation of Land Bridge.'

'Can such information be easily transferred from temporary storage to permanent?' I asked.

'Easily, yes. Everything is electromagnetic here. Our facts are aggregates of charges; we shift them from brain to brain by reversing polarities.'

'What if there were an electrical failure?' I demanded. 'You say you have no redundancy here. Is there no possibility of losing data through some accident?'

'None,' said the guide smoothly. 'We have a series of fallback devices to insure continuity of power. And by using organic tissue for our storage cells, we have the best assurance of safety of all: for the brains themselves will retain their data in the event of a power interruption. It would be taxing but not impossible to recapture their contents.'

'During the invasion,' I said, 'were difficulties experienced?'

'We are under the protection of the invaders, who regard our work as vital to their own interests.'

Not long afterward, at a general convocation of the Rememberers, we apprentices were permitted to look on from a balcony of the guildhall; below us, in full majesty, were the guild members, shawls in place, Elegro and Olmayne among them. On a dais that bore the helical symbol was Chancellor Kenishal of the Rememberers, an austere and commanding figure, and beside him was an even more conspicuous personage who was of the species that had conquered Earth. Kenishal spoke briefly. The resonance of his voice did not entirely conceal ths hollowness of his words; like all administrators everywhere, he gushed platitudes, praising himself by implication as he congratulated his guild for its notable work. Then he introduced the invader.

The alien stretched forth his arms until they seemed to touch the walls of the auditorium.

'I am Manrule Seven,' he said quietly. 'I am Procurator of Perris, with particular responsibility for the guild of Rememberers. My purpose here today is to confirm the decree of the provisional occupational government. You Rememberers are to go totally unhampered in your work. You are to have free access to all sites on this planet or on any other planet or on any other world that may have bearing on your mastery of the past of this planet. All files are to remain open to you, except those pertaining to the organization of the conquest itself. Chancellor Kenishal has informed me that the conquest lies outside the scope of your present research in any case, so no hardship will be worked. We of the occupying government are aware of the value of the work of your guild. The history of this planet is of great significance, and we wish your efforts continued.'

'To make Earth a better tourist attraction,' said the Prince of Roum bitterly at my side.

Manrule Seven went on, 'The Chancellor has requested me to inform you of one administrative change that will necessarily follow from the occupied status of your planet. In the past, all disputes among you were settled by the courts of your own guild, with Chancellor Kenishal having the highest right of appeal. For the sake of efficient administration it now becomes mandatory for us to impose our jurisdiction over that of the guild. Therefore the Chancellor will transfer to us those litigations which he feels no longer fall into his sphere of authority.'

The Rememberers gasped. There was a sudden shifting of postures and exchanging of glances on the floor below.

'The Chancellor's abdicating!' blurted an apprentice near me.'

'What choice does he have, fool?' another whispered harshly.

The meeting broke up in some confusion. Rememberers flooded into the hallways, gesticulating, debating, expostulating. One venerable wearer of the shawl was so shaken that he crouched down and began to make the series of stabilizer responses, heedless of the throng. The tide swept over us apprentices, forcing us back. I attempted to protect the Prince, fearing that he would be thrown to the floor and trampled; but we were swept apart and I lost sight of him for minutes. When I saw him again he stood with the Rememberer Olmayne. Her face was flushed, her eyes were bright; she was speaking rapidly, and the Prince was listening. His hand clung to her elbow as if for support.

4

After the conclusion of the early period of orientations, I was given trivial tasks. Chiefly I was asked to do things that in an earlier time would have been performed wholly by machine: for example, to monitor the feed lines that oozed nutrients into the brain-boxes of the memory tanks. For several hours each day I walked through the narrow corridor of the inspection panels, searching for clogged lines. It had been so devised that when a line became blocked, a stress pattern was created the length of the clear tubing that contained it, and beams of a special polarised light illuminated that pattern for benefit of the inspector. I did my humble task, now and again finding a blockage, and I did other little jobs as befitted my status of apprenticeship.

However, I also had the opportunity to pursue my own investigations into the events of my planet's past.

Sometimes one does not learn the value of things until they are lost. For a lifetime I served as a Watcher, striving to give early warning of a promised invasion of Earth, while caring little who might wish to invade us, or why. For a lifetime I realised dimly that Earth had known grander days than those of the Third Cycle into which I had been born, and yet I sought no knowledge of what those days had been like and of the reasons of our present diminished condition. Only when the starships of the invaders blossomed in the sky did I feel a sudden hunger to know of that lost past. Now, as the most elderly of apprentices, I, Tomis of the Rememberers rummaged through the archives of vanished time.

Any citizen has the right to go to a public thinking cap and requisition an information from the Rememberers on any given subject. Nothing is concealed. But the Rememberers volunteer no aid; you must know how to ask, which means you must know what to ask. Item by item you must seek your facts. It is useful for those who must know, say, the long-term patterns of climate in Agupt, or the symbols

93

of the crystallisation disease, or the limitations in the charter of one of the guilds; but it is no help at all to the man who wishes knowledge of the larger questions. One would need to requisition a thousand informations merely to make a beginning. The expense would be great; few would bother.

As an apprentice Rememberer I had full access to all data. More important, I had access to the indexes. The Indexers are a guild subsidiary to the Rememberers, a donkey-guild of drudges who record and classify that which they often do not understand; the end product of their toil serves the greater guild, but the indexes are not open to all. Without them one scarcely is able to cope with the problems of research. I will not summarise the stages by which I came by my knowledge – the hours spent shuffling through inter-woven corridors, the rebuffs, the bewilderments, the throbbing of the brain. As a foolish novice I was at the mercy of pranksters, and many a fellow apprentice, even a guild member or two, led me astray for the sheer wicked joy of it. But I learned which routes to follow, how to set up sequences of questions, how to follow a path of references higher and higher until the truth bursts dazzlingly upon one. With persistence rather than with great intellect I wrung from the files of the Rememberers a coherent tale of the downfall of man.

This:

There was a time in ages past when life on Earth was brutal and primitive. We call this time the First Cycle. I do not speak of the period before civilisation, that time of grunting and hairiness, of caves and stone tools. We consider the First Cycle to have commenced when man first learned to record information and to control environment. This occurred in Agupt and Sumir. By our way of reckoning the First Cycle commenced some 40,000 years ago – however, we are uncertain of its true length in its own terms, since the span of the year was altered at the end of the Second Cycle, and we have been unable thus far to determine how long, in previous eras, it took for our world to circle its sun. Somewhat longer than at present, perhaps.

The First Cycle was the time of Imperial Roum and of the first flowering of Jorslem. Eyrop remained savage long after Ais and parts of Afreek were civilised. In the west, two great continents occupied much of Earth Ocean, and these too were held by savages.

It is understood that in this cycle mankind had no contact with other worlds or stars. Such solitude is difficult to comprehend, but yet so it occurred. Mankind had no way of creating light except through fire; he could not cure his ills; life was not susceptible to renewal. It was a time without comforts, a gay time, harsh in its simplicity. Death came early; one barely had time to scatter a few sons about, and one was carried off. One lived with fear, but mostly not fear of real things.

The soul recoils from such an era. But yet it is true that in the First Cycle magnificent cities were founded – Roum, Perris, Atin, Jorslem – and splendid deeds were accomplished. One stands in awe of those ancestors, foul-smelling (no doubt), illiterate, without machines, and still capable of coming to terms with their universe and to some extent of mastering it.

War and grief were constant throughout the First Cycle. Destruction and creation were nearly simultaneous. Flames ate man's most glorious cities. Chaos threatened always to engulf order. How could men have endured such conditions for thousands of years?

Towards the close of the First Cycle much of the primitivism was outgrown. At last sources of power were accessible to man; there was the beginning of true transportation; communications over distances became possible; many inventions transformed the world in a short time. Methods of making war kept pace with the technological growth in other directions; but total catastrophe was averted, although several times it appeared to have arrived. It was during the final phase of the cycle that the Lost Continents were colonised, also Stralya, and that first contact was made with the adjoining planets of our solar system.

The transition from First Cycle to Second is arbitarily fixed at the point when man first encountered intelligent beings from distant worlds. This, the Rememberers now believe, took place less than fifty generations after the First Cycle folk had mastered electronic and nuclear energy. Thus we may rightly say that the early people of Earth stumbled headlong from savagery to galactic contact – or, perhaps, that they crossed that gap in a few quick strides.

This too is cause for pride. For if the First Cycle was great despite its handicaps, the Second Cycle knew of no handicaps and achieved miracles.

In this epoch mankind spread out to the stars, and the stars came to mankind. Earth was a market for goods of all worlds. Wonders were commonplace. One might hope to live for hundreds of years; eyes, hearts, lungs, kidneys were replaced as easily as shoes; the air was pure, no man went hungry, war was forgotten. Machines of every sort served man. But the machines were not enough, and so the Second Cycle folk bred men who were machines, or machines who were men: creatures that were genetically human, but were born artificially, and were treated with drugs that prevented the permanent storing of memories. These creatures, analogous to our neuters, were capable of performing an efficient day's work, but were unable to build up that permanent body of experiences, memories, expectations, and abilities that is the mark of a human soul. Millions of such not-quite humans handled the duller tasks of the day, freeing others for lives of glistening fulfilment. After the creation of the subhumans came the creation of the superanimals who, through biochemical manipulation of the brain, were able to carry out tasks once beyond the capacity of their species: dogs, cats, mice, and cattle were enrolled in the labour force, while certain high primates received functions formerly reserved for humans. Through this exploitation of the environment to the fullest, man created a paradise on Earth.

The spirit of man soared to the loftiest peak it had known. Poets, scholars, and scientists made splendid contributions. Shining cities sprawled across the land. The population was enormous, and even so, there was ample room for all, with no shortage of resources. One could indulge one's whims to any extent; there was much experimentation with genetic surgery and with mutagenetic and teratogenetic drugs, so that the human species adopted many new forms. There was, however, nothing yet like the variant forms of our cycle.

Across the sky in stately procession moved space stations serving every imaginable need. It was at this time that the two new moons were built, although the Rememberers have not yet determined whether their purpose was functional or esthetic. The auroras that now appear each night in the sky may have been installed at this time, although some factions of Rememberers argue that the presence of temperate-zone auroras began with the geophysical upheavals that heralded the close of the cycle.

It was, at any rate, the finest of times to be alive.

'See earth and die,' was the watchword of the outworlders. No one making the galactic grand tour dared pass up this planet of miracles. We welcomed the strangers, accepted their compliments and their money, made them comfortable in the ways they preferred, and proudly displayed our greatnesses.

The Prince of Roum can testify that it is the fate of the mighty eventually to be humbled, and also that the higher one reaches for splendour, the more catastrophic one's downfall is apt to be. After some thousands of years of glories beyond my capacity to comprehend, the fortunate ones of the Second Cycle overreached themselves and committed two misdeeds, one born of foolish arrogance, the other born of excessive confidence. Earth is paying yet for those overreachings.

The effects of the first were slow to be felt. It was a function of Earth's attitude toward the other species of the galaxy, which had shifted during the Second Cycle from awe to matter-of-fact acceptance to contempt. At the beginning of the cycle, brash and naive Earth had erupted into a galaxy already peopled by advanced races that long had been in contact with one another. This could well have produced a soul-crushing trauma, but instead it generated an aggressive urge to excel and surpass. And so it happened that Earthmen quickly came to look upon most of the galactics as equals, and then, as progress continued on Earth, as inferiors. This bred the easy habit of contempt for the backward.

Thus it was proposed to establish 'study compounds' on Earth for specimens of inferior races. These compounds would reproduce the natural habitat of the races and would be accessible to scholars wishing to observe the life-processes of these races. However, the expense of collecting and maintaining the specimens was such that it quickly became necessary to open the compounds to the public at large, for purposes of amusement. These supposedly scientific compounds were, in fact, zoos for other intelligent species.

At the outset only the truly alien beings were collected, those so remote from human biological or psychological norms that there was little danger of regarding them as 'people.' A many-limbed being that dwells in a tank of methane under high pressure does not strike a sympathetic response from those likely to object to the captivity of intelligent creatures. If that methane-dweller happens to have a complex civilization of a sort uniquely fitted to its environment, it can be argued that it is all the more important to duplicate that environment on Earth so that one can study so strange a civilization. Therefore the early compounds contained only the bizarre. The collectors were limited, also, to taking creatures who had not attained the stage of galactic travel themselves. It would not have been good form to kidnap life-forms whose relatives were among the interstellar tourists on whom our world's economy had come so heavily to depend.

The success of the first compounds led to the demand for the formation of others. Less critical standards were imposed; not merely the utterly alien and grotesque were collected, but samplings of any sort of galactic life not in a position to register diplomatic protests. And, as the audacity of our ancestors increased, so did the restrictions on collection loosen, until there were samplings from a thousand worlds on Earth, including some whose civilizations were older and more intricate than our own.

The archives of the Rememberers show that the expansion of our compounds stirred some agitation in many parts of the universe. We were denounced as marauders, kidnappers, and pirates; committees were formed to criticize our wanton disregard for the rights of sentient beings; Earthmen travelling to other planets were occasionally beset by mobs of hostile life-forms demanding that we free the prisoners of the compounds at once. However, these protesters were only a minority – most galactics kept an uncomfortable silence about our compounds. They regretted the barbarity of them, and nevertheless made a point of touring them when they visited Earth. Where else, after all, could one see hundreds of life-forms, culled from every part of the universe, in a few days? Our compounds were a major attraction, one of the wonders of the cosmos. By silent conspiracy our neighbors in the galaxy winked at the amorality of the basic concept in order to share the pleasure of inspecting the prisoners.

There is in the archives of the Rememberers a memory-tank entry of a visit to a compound area. It is one of the oldest visual records possessed by the guild, and I obtained a look at it only with great difficulty and upon the direct intercession of the Remembrancer Olmayne. Despite the use of a double filter in the cap, one sees the scene only blurredly; but yet it is clear enough. Behind a curved shield of a transparent material are fifty or more beings of an unnamed world. Their bodies are pyramidial, with dark blue surfaces and pink visual areas at each vertex; they walk upon short, thick legs; they have one pair of grasping limbs on each face. Though it is risky to attempt to interpret the inner feelings of extraterrestrial beings, one can clearly sense a mood of utter despair in these creatures. Through the murky green gases of their environment they move slowly, numbly, without animation. Several have joined tips in what must be communication. One appears newly dead. Two are bowed to the ground like tumbled toys, but their limbs move in what perhaps is prayer. It is a dismal scene. Later, I discovered other such records in neglected corners of the building. They taught me much.

For more than a thousand Second Cycle years the growth of these compounds continued unchecked, until it came to seem logical and natural to all except the victims that Earth should practice these cruelties in the name of science. Then, upon a distant world not previously visited by Earthmen, there were discovered certain beings of a primitive kind, comparable perhaps to Earthmen in early First Cycle days. These beings were roughly humanoid in form, undeniably intelligent, and fiercely savage. At the loss of several Earth-born lives, a collecting team acquired a breeding colony of these people and transported them to Earth to be placed in a compound.

This was the first of the Second Cycle's two fatal errors.

At the time of the kidnapping, the beings of this other world – which is never named in the records, but known only by the code designation H362 – were in no position to protest or to take punitive steps. But shortly they were visited by emissaries from certain other worlds aligned politically against Earth. Under the guidance of these emissaries, the beings of H362 requested the return of their people. Earth refused, citing the long precedent of interstallar condonement of the compounds. Lengthy diplomatic representations followed, in the course of which Earth simply reaffirmed its right to have acted in such a fashion.

The people of H362 responded with threats. 'One day,' they said, 'we will cause you to regret this. We will invade and conquer your planet, set free all the inhabitants of the compounds, and turn Earth itself into a gigantic compound for its own people.'

Under the circumstances this appeared quite amusing.

Little more was heard of the outraged inhabitants of H362 over the next few millennia. They were progressing rapidly, in their distant part of the universe, but since by all calculations it would take them a cosmic period to pose any menace to Earth, they were ignored. How could one fear spear-wielding savages?

Earth addressed itself to a new challenge: full control of the planetary climate.

Weather modification had been practiced on a small scale since late First Cycle. Clouds holding potential rain could be induced to release it; fogs could be dispelled; hail could be made less destructive. Certain steps were taken toward reducing the polar ice packs and toward making deserts more fruitful. However, these measurers were strictly local and, with few exceptions, had no lasting effects on environment.

The Second Cycle endeavor involved the erection of enormous columns at more than one hundred locations around the globe. We do not know the heights of these columns, since none has survived intact and the specifications are lost, but it is thought that they equaled or exceeded the highest buildings previously constructed, and perhaps attained altitudes of two miles or more. Within these columns was equipment which was designed, among other things, to effect displacements of the poles of Earth's magnetic field.

As we understand the aim of the weather machines, it was to modify the planet's geography according to a carefully conceived plan arising from the division of what we call Earth Ocean into a number of large bodies. Although interconnected, these suboceans were considered to have

100

individual existences, since along most of their boundary region they were cut off from the rest of Earth Ocean by land masses. In the northern Lost Continent (known as Usa-amrik) in the west and the proximity of Usa-amrik to Eyrop in the east left only narrow straits through which the polar waters could mingle with those of the warmer oceans flanking the Lost Continents.

Manipulation of magnetic forces produced a libration of Earth on its orbit, calculated to break up the north polar ice pack and permit the cold water trapped by this pack to come in contact with warmer water from elsewhere. By removing the northern ice pack and thus exposing the northern ocean to evaporation, precipitation would be greatly increased there. To prevent this precipitation from falling in the north as snow, additional manipulations were to be induced to change the pattern of the prevailing westerly winds which carried precipitation over temperate areas. A natural conduit was to be established that would bring the precipitation of the polar region to areas in lower latitudes lacking in proper moisture.

There was much more to the plan than this. Our knowledge of the details is hazy. We are aware of schemes to shift ocean currents by causing land subsidence or emergence, of proposals to deflect solar heat from the tropics to the poles, and of other rearrangements. The details are unimportant. What is significant to us are the consequences of this grandoise plan.

After a period of preparation lasting centuries and after absorbing more effort and wealth than any other project in human history, the weather machines were put into operation.

The result was devastation.

The disastrous experiment in planetary alteration resulted in a shifting of the geographical poles, a lengthy period of glacial conditions throughout most of the northern hemisphere, the unexpected submergence of Usa-amrik and Sud-amrik, its neighbor, the creation of Land Bridge joining Afreek and Eyrop, and the near destruction of human civilization. These upheavals did not take place with great speed. Evidently the project went smoothly for the first several centuries; the polar ice thawed, and the corresponding rise in sea levels was dealt with by constructing fusion evapor-

101

ators – small suns, in effect – at selected oceanic points. Only slowly did it become clear that the weather machines were bringing about architectonic changes in the crust of Earth. These, unlike the climatic changes, proved irreversible.

It was a time of furious storms followed by unending droughts; of the loss of hundreds of millions of lives; of the disruption of all communications; of panicky mass migrations out of the doomed continents. Chaos triumphed. The splendid civilization of the Second Cycle was shattered. The compounds of alien life were destroyed.

For the sake of saving what remained of its population, several of the most powerful galactic races took command of our planet. They established energy pylons to stabilize Earth's axial wobble; they dismantled those weather machines that had not been destroyed by the planetary convulsions; they fed the hungry, clothed the naked, and offered reconstruction loans. For us it was a Time of Sweeping, when all the structures and conventions of society were expunged. No longer masters in our own world, we accepted the charity of strangers and crept pitifully about.

Yet, because we were still the same race we had been, we recovered to some extent. We had squandered our planet's capital and so could never again be anything but bankrupts and paupers, but in a humbler way we entered into our Third Cycle. Certain scientific techniques of earlier days still remained to us. Others were devised, working generally on different principles. Our guilds were formed to give order to society: Dominators, Master, Merchants, and the rest. The Rememberers strove to salvage what could be pulled from the wreck of the past.

Our debts to our rescuers were enormous. As bankrupts, we had no way of repaying those debts; we hoped instead for a quitclaim, a statement of absolution. Negotiations to that effect were already under way when an unexpected intervention occurred. The inhabitants of H362 approached the committee of Earth's receivers and offered to reimburse them for their expenses — in return for an assignment of all rights and claims in Earth to H362.

It was done.

H362 now regarded itself the owner by treaty of our world. It served notice to the universe at large that it reserved the right to take possession at any future date. As

102

well it might, since at that time H362 was still incapable of interstellar travel. Thereafter, though, H362 was deemed legal possessor of the assets of Earth, as purchaser in bankruptcy.

No one failed to realize that this was H362's way of fulfilling its threat to 'turn Earth itself into a gigantic compound,' as revenge for the injury inflicted by our collecting team long before.

On Earth, Third Cycle society constituted itself along the lines it now holds, with its rigid stratification of guilds. The threat of H362 was taken seriously, for ours was a chastened world that sneered at no menace, however slight; and a guild of Watchers was devised to scan the skies for attackers. Defenders and all the rest followed. In some small ways we demonstrated our old flair for imagination, particularly in the Years of Magic, when a fanciful impulse created the self-perpetuating mutant guild of Fliers, a parallel guild of Swimmers, of whom little is heard nowadays, and several other varieties, including a troublesome and unpredictable guild of Changelings whose genetic characteristics were highly erratic.

The Watchers watched. The Dominators ruled. The Fliers soared. Life went on, year after year, in Eyrop and in Ais, in Stralya, in Afreek, in the scattered islands that were the only remnants of the Lost Continents of Usa-amrik and Sud-amrik. The vow of H362 receded into mythology, but yet we remained vigilant. And far across the cosmos our enemies gathered strength, attaining some measure of the power that had been ours in our Second Cycle. They never forgot the day when their kinsmen had been held captive in our compounds.

In a night of terror they came to us. Now they are our masters, and their vow is fulfilled, their claim asserted.

All this, and much more, I learned as I burrowed in the accumulated knowledge of the guild of Rememberers.

5

Meanwhile the former Prince of Roum was wantonly abusing the hospitality of our co-sponsorer, the Rememberer Elegro. I should have been aware of what was going on, for I knew the Prince and his ways better than any other man in Perris. But I was too busy in the archives, learning of the past. While I explored the details of the Second Cycle's protoplasm files and regeneration nodules, its time-wind blowers and its photonic-flue fixers, Prince Enric was seducing the Rememberer Olmayne.

Like most seductions, I imagine that this was no great contest of wills. Olmayne was a woman of sensuality, whose attitude toward her husband was affectionate but patronizing. She regarded Elegro openly as ineffectual, a bumbler; and Elegro, whose haughtiness and stern mien did not conceal his underlying weakness of purpose, seemed to merit her disdain. What kind of marriage they had was not my business to observe, but clearly she was the stronger, and just as clearly he could not meet her demands.

Then, too, why had Olmayne agreed to sponsor us into her guild?

Surely not out of any desire for a tattered old Watcher. It must have been the wish to know more of the strange and oddly commanding blind Pilgrim who was that Watcher's companion. From the very first, then, Olmayne must have been drawn to Prince Enric; and he, naturally, would need little encouragement to accept the gift she offered.

Possibly they were lovers almost from the moment of our arrival in the Hall of Rememberers.

I went my way, and Elegro went his, and Olmayne and Prince Enric went theirs, and summer gave way to autumn and autumn to winter. I excavated the records with passionate impatience. Never before had I known such involvement, such intensity of curiosity. Without benefit of a visit to Jorslem I felt renewed. I saw the Prince infrequently, and our meetings were generally silent; it was not my place to question him about his doings, and he felt no wish to volunteer information to me.

Occasionally I thought of my former life, and of my travels from place to place, and of the Flier Avluela who was now, I supposed, the consort of one of our conquerors. How did the false Changeling Gormon style himself, now that he had emerged from his disguise and owned himself to be one of those from H362? Earthking Nine? Oceanlord Five? Overman Three? Wherever he was, he must feel satisfaction, I thought, at the total success of the conquest of Earth.

Toward winter's end I learned of the affair between the Rememberer Olmayne and Prince Enric of Roum. I picked up whispered gossip in the apprentice quarters first; then I noticed the smiles on the faces of other Rememberers when Elegro and Olmayne were about; lastly, I observed the behavior of the Prince and Olmayne toward one another. It was obvious. Those touchings of hand to hand, those sly exchanges of catchwords and private phrases – what else could they mean?'

Among the Rememberers the marriage vow is regarded solemnly. As with Fliers, mating is for life, and one is not supposed to betray one's partner as Olmayne was doing. When one is married to a fellow Rememberer – a custom in the guild, but not universal – the union is all the more sacred.

What revenge would Elegro take when in time he learned the truth?

It happened that I was present when the situation at last crystallized into conflict. It was a night in earliest spring. I had worked long and hard in the deepest pits of the memory tanks, prying forth data that no one had bothered with since it had first been stored; and, with my head aswim with images of chaos, I walked through the glow of the Perris night, seeking fresh air. I strolled along the Senn and was accosted by an agent for a Somnambulist, who offered to sell me insight into the world of dreams. I came upon a lone Pilgrim at his devotions before a temple of flesh. I watched a pair of young Fliers in passage overhead, and shed a self-pitying tear or two. I was halted by a starborn tourist in breathing mask and jeweled tunic; he

105

put his cratered red face close to mine and vented hallucinations in my nostrils. At length I returned to the Hall of Rememberers and went to the suite of my sponsors to pay my respects before retiring.

Olmayne and Elegro were there. So, too, was Prince Enric. Olmayne admitted me with a quick gesture of one fingertip, but took no further notice of me, nor did the others. Elegro was tensely pacing the floor, stomping about so vehemently that the delicate life-forms of the carpet folded and unfolded their petals in wild agitation.. 'A Pilgrim!' Elegro cried. 'If it had been some trash of a Vendor, it would only be humiliating. But a Pilgrim? That makes it monstrous!'

Prince Enric stood with arms folded, body motionless. It was impossible to detect the expression beneath his mask of Pilgrimage, but he appeared wholly calm.

Elegro said, 'Will you deny that you have been tampering with the sanctity of my pairing?'

'I deny nothing. I assert nothing.'

'And you?' Elegro demanded, whirling on his lady. 'Speak truth, Olmayne! For once, speak truth! What of the stories they tell of you and this Pilgrim?'

'I have heard no stories,' said Olmayne sweetly.

'That he shares your bed! That you taste potions together! That you travel to ecstasy together!'

Olmayne's smile did not waver. Her broad face was tranquil. To me she looked more beautiful than ever.

Elegro tugged in anguish at the strands of his shawl. His dour, bearded face darkened in wrath and exasperation. His hand slipped within his tunic and emerged with the tiny glossy bead of a vision capsule, which he thrust forth toward the guilty pair on the palm of his hand.

'Why should I waste breath?' he asked. 'Everything is here. The full record in the photonic flux. You have been under surveillance. Did either of you think anything could be hidden here, of all places? You, Olmayne, a Rememberer, how could you think so?'

Olmayne examined the capsule from a distance, as though it were a primed implosion bomb. With distaste she said, 'How like you to spy on us, Elegro. Did it give you great pleasure to watch us in our joy?'

'Beast!' he cried.

Pocketing the capsule, he advanced toward the motionless Prince. Elegro's face was now contorted with righteous wrath. Standing at arm's length from the Prince he declared icily, 'You will be punished to the fullest for this impiety. You will be stripped of your Pilgrim's robes and delivered up to the fate reserved for monsters. The Will shall consume your soul!'

Prince Enric replied, 'Curb your tongue.'

'Curb my tongue? Who are you to speak that way? A Pilgrim who lusts for the wife of his host – who doubly violates holiness – who drips lies and sanctimony at the same moment?' Elegro frothed. His iciness was gone. Now he ranted in nearly incoherent frenzy, displaying his interior weakness by his lack of self-control. We three stood frozen, astounded by his torrent of words, and at last the stasis broke when the Rememberer, carried away by the tide of his own indignation, seized the Prince by the shoulders and began violently to shake him.

'Filth,' Enric bellowed, 'you may not put your hands to me!'

With a double thrust of his fists against Elegro's chest he hurled the Rememberer reeling backward across the room. Elegro crashed into a suspension cradle and sent a flank of watery artifacts tumbling; three flasks of scintillating fluids shivered and spilled their contents; the carpet set up a shrill cry of pained protest. Gasping, stunned, Elegro pressed a hand to his breast and looked to us for assistance.

'Physical assault—' Elegro wheezed. 'A shameful crime!'

'The first assault was your doing,' Olmayne reminded her husband.

Pointing trembling fingers, Elegro muttered, 'For this there can be no forgiveness, Pilgrim!'

'Call me Pilgrim no longer,' Enric said. His hands went to the grillwork of his mask. Olmayne cried out, trying to prevent him; but in his anger the Prince knew no check. He hurled the mask to the floor and stood with his harsh face terribly exposed, the cruel features hawk-lean, the gray mechanical spheres in his eyesockets masking the depths of his fury. 'I am the Prince of Roum,' he announced in a voice of thunder. 'Down and abase! Down and abase! Quick, Rememberer, the three prostrations and five abasements!'

107

Elegro appeared to crumble. He peered in disbelief; then he sagged, and in a kind of reflex of amazement he performed a ritual obeisance before his wife's seducer. It was the first time since the fall of Roum that the Prince had asserted his former status, and the pleasure of it was so evident on his ravaged face that even the blank eyeballs appeared to glow in regal pride.

'Out,' the Prince ordered. 'Leave us.'

Elegro fled.

I remained, astounded, staggered. The Prince nodded courteously to me. 'Would you pardon us, old friend, and grant us some moments of privacy?'

6

A WEAK man can be put to rout by a surprise attack, but afterward he pauses, reconsiders, and hatches schemes. So was it with the Rememberer Elegro. Driven from his own suite by the unmasking of the Prince of Roum, he grew calm and crafty once he was out of that terrifying presence. Later that same night, as I settled into my sleeping cradle and debated aiding slumber with a drug, Elegro summoned me to his research cell on a lower level of the building.

There he sat amid the paraphernalia of his guild: reels and spools, data-flakes, capsules, caps, a quartet of series-linked skulls, a row of output screens, a small ornamental helix, all the symbology of the gatherers of information. In his hands he grasped a tension-draining crystal from one of the Cloud-worlds; its milky interior was rapidly tingeing with sepia as it pulled anxieties from his spirit. He pretended a look of stern authority, as if forgetting that I had seen him exposed in his spinelessness.

He said, 'Were you aware of this man's identity when you came with him to Perris?'

'Yes.'

'You said nothing about it.'

'I was never asked.'

'Do you know what a risk you have exposed all of us to, by causing us unknowingly to harbor a Dominator?'

'We are Earthmen,' I said. 'Do we not still acknowledge the authority of the Dominators?'

'Not since the conquest. By decree of the invaders all former governments are dissolved and their leaders subject to arrest.'

'But surely we should resist such an order!'

The Rememberer Elegro regarded me quizzically. 'Is it a Rememberer's function to meddle in politics? Tomis, we obey the government in power, whichever it may be and however it may have taken control. We conduct no resistance activities here.'

'I see.'

'Therefore we must rid ourselves at once of this dangerous fugitive. Tomis, I instruct you to go at once to occupation headquarters and inform Manrule Seven that we have captured the Prince of Roum and hold him here for pickup.'

'*I* should go?' I blurted. 'Why send an old man as a messenger in the night? An ordinary thinking-cap transmission would be enough!'

'Too risky. Strangers may intercept cap communications. It would not go well for our guild if this were spread about. This has to be a personal communication.'

'But to choose an unimportant apprentice to carry it – it seems strange.'

'There are only two of us who know,' said Elegro. 'I will not go. Therefore you must.'

'With no introduction to Manrule Seven I will never be admitted.'

'Inform his aides that you have information leading to the apprehension of the Prince of Roum. You'll be heard.

'Am I to mention your name?'

'If necessary. You may say that the Prince is being held prisoner in my quarters with the cooperation of my wife.'

I nearly laughed at that. But I held a straight face before this cowardly Rememberer, who did not even dare to go himself and denounce the man who had cuckolded him.

'Ultimately,' I said, 'the Prince will become aware of what we have done. Is it right of you to ask me to betray a man who was my companion for so many months?'

'It is not a matter of betrayal. It is a matter of obligations to the government.'

'I feel no obligation to this government. My loyalties are to the guild of Dominators. Which is why I gave assistance to the Prince of Roum in his moment of peril.'

'For that,' said Elegro, 'your own life could be forfeit to our conquerors. Your only expiation is to admit your error and cooperate in bringing about his arrest. Go. Now.'

In a long and tolerant life I have never despised anyone so vehemently as I did the Rememberer Elegro at that moment.

Yet I saw that I was faced with few choices, none of them palatable. Elegro wished his undoer punished, but lacked the courage to report him himself; therefore I must give over to the conquering authorities one whom I had sheltered and assisted, and for whom I felt a responsibility. If I refused, Elegro would perhaps hand me to the invaders for punishment myself, as an accessory to the Prince's escape from Roum; or he might take vengeance against me within the machinery of the guild of Rememberers. If I obliged Elegro, though, I would have a stain on my conscience forever, and in the event of a restoration of the power of the Dominators I would have much to answer for.

As I weighed the possibilities, I triply cursed the Rememberer Elegro's faithless wife and her invertebrate husband.

I hesitated a bit. Elegro offered more persuasion, threatening to arraign me before the guild on such charges as unlawfully gaining access to secret files and improperly introducing into guild precincts a proscribed fugitive. He threatened to cut me off forever from the information pool. He spoke vaguely of vengeance.

In the end I told him I would go to the invaders' headquarters and do his bidding. I had by then conceived a betrayal that would – I hoped – cancel the betrayal Elegro was enforcing on me.

Dawn was near when I left the building. The air was mild and sweet; a low mist hung over the streets of Perris, giving them a gentle shimmer. No moons were in sight. In the deserted streets I felt uneasy, although I told myself that no one would care to do harm to an aged Rememberer; but I was armed only with a small blade, and I feared bandits.

My route lay on one of the pedestrian ramps. I panted a bit at the steep incline, but when I had attained the proper level I was more secure, since here there were patrol nodes at frequent intervals, and here, too, were some other late-night strollers. I passed a spectral figure garbed in white satin through which Alien features peered: a revenant, a ghostly inhabitant of a planet of the Bull, where reincarnation is the custom and no man goes about installed in his own original body. I passed three female beings of a Swan planet who giggled at me and asked if I had seen males of their species, since the time of conjugation was upon them. I passed a pair of Changelings who eyed me speculatively, decided I had nothing on me worth robbing, and moved

111

on, their piebald dewlaps jiggling and their radiant skins flashing like beacons.

At last I came to the squat octagonal building occupied by the Procurator of Perris.

It was indifferently guarded. The invaders appeared confident that we were incapable of mounting a counter-assault against them, and quite likely they were right; a planet which can be conquered between darkness and dawn is not going to launch a plausible resistance afterwards. Around the building rose the pale glow of a protective scanner. There was a tinge of ozone in the air. In the wide plaza across the way, Merchants were setting up their market for the morning; I saw barrels of spices being unloaded by brawny Servitors, and dark sausages carried by files of neuters. I stepped through the scanner beam and an invader emerged to challenge me.

I explained that I carried urgent news for Manrule Seven, and in short order, with amazingly little consultation of intermediaries, I was ushered into the Procurator's presence.

The invader had furnished his office simply but in good style. It was decked entirely with Earthmade objects: a drapery from Afreek weave, two alabaster pots from ancient Agupt, a marble statuette that might have been early Roumish, and a dark Talyan vase in which a few wilting deathflowers languished. When I entered, he seemed preoccupied with several message-cubes; as I had heard, the invaders did most of their work in the dark hours, and it did not surprise me to find him so busy now. After a moment he loked up and said, 'What is it, old man? What's this about a fugitive Dominator?'

'The Prince of Roum,' I said. 'I know of his location.'

At once his cold eyes sparkled with interest. He ran his many-fingered hands across his desk, on which were mounted the emblems of several of our guilds, Transporters and Rememberers and Defenders and Clowns, among others. 'Go on,' he said.

'The Prince is in this city. He is in a specific place and has no way of escaping from it.'

'And you are here to inform me of his location?'

'No,' I said. 'I'm here to buy his liberty.'

Manrule Seven seemed perplexed. 'There are times when

112

you humans baffle me. You say you've captured this runaway Dominator, and I assume that you want to sell him to us, but you say you want to *buy* him. Why bother coming to us? Is this a joke?'

'Will you permit an explanation?'

He brooded into the mirrored top of his desk while I told him in a compressed way of my journey from Roum with the blinded Prince, of our arrival at the Hall of Rememberers, of Prince Enric's seduction of Olmayne, and of Elegro's petty, fuming desire for vengeance. I made it clear that I had come to the invaders only under duress and that it was not my intention to betray the Prince into their hands. Then I said, 'I realize that all Dominators are forfeit to you. Yet this one has already paid a high price for his freedom. I ask you to notify the Rememberers that the Prince of Roum is under amnesty, and to permit him to continue on as a Pilgrim to Jorslem. In that way Elegro will lose power over him.'

'What is it that you offer us,' asked Manrule Seven, 'in return for this amnesty for your Prince?'

'I have done research in the memory tanks of the Rememberers.'

'And?'

'I have found that for which your people have been seeking.'

Manrule Seven studied me with care. 'How would you have any idea of what we seek?'

'There is in the deepest part of the Hall of Rememberers,' I said quietly, 'an image recording of the compound in which your kidnapped ancestors lived while they were prisoners on Earth. It shows their sufferings in poignant detail. It is a superb justification for the conquest of Earth by H362.'

'Impossible! There's no such document!'

From the intensity of the invader's reaction, I knew that I had stung him in the vulnerable place.

He went on, 'We've searched your files thoroughly. There's only one recording of compound life, and it doesn't show our people. It shows a nonhumanoid pyramid-shaped race, probably from one of the Anchor worlds.'

'I have seen that one,' I told him. 'There are others. I spent many hours searching for them, out of hunger to know of our past injustices.'

113

'The indexes—'

'—are sometimes incomplete. I found this recording only by accident. The Rememberers themselves have no idea it's there. I'll lead you to it – if you agree to leave the Prince of Roum unmolested.'

The Procurator was silent a moment. At length he said, 'You puzzle me. I am unable to make out if you are a scoundrel or a man of the highest virtue.'

'I know where true loyalty lies.'

'To betray the secrets of your guild, though—'

'I am no Rememberer, only an apprentice, formerly a Watcher. I would not have you harm the Prince at the wish of a cuckolded fool. The Prince is in his hands; only you can obtain his release now. And so I must offer you this document.'

'Which the Rememberers have carefully deleted from their indexes, so it will not fall into our hands.'

'Which the Rememberers have carelessly misplaced and forgotten.'

'I doubt it,' said Manrule Seven. 'They are not careless folk. They hid that recording; and by giving it to us, are you not betraying all your world? Making yourself a collaborator with the hated enemy?'

I shrugged. 'I am interested in having the Prince of Roum made free. Other means and ends are of no concern to me. The location of the document is yours in exchange for the grant of amnesty.'

The invader displayed what might have been his equivalent of a smile. 'It is not in our best interests to allow members of the former guild of Dominators to remain at large. Your position is precarious, do you see? I could extract the document's location from you by force – and still have the Prince as well.'

'So you could,' I agreed. 'I take that risk. I assume a certain basic honor among people who came to avenge an ancient crime. I am in your power, and the whereabouts of the document is in my mind, yours for the picking.'

Now he laughed in an unmistakable show of good humor.

'Wait a moment,' he said. He spoke a few words of his own language into an amber communication device, and shortly a second member of his species entered the office. I recognized him instantly, although he was shorn of some

114

of the flamboyant disguise he had worn when he traveled with me as Gormon, the supposed Changeling. He offered the ambivalent smile of his kind and said, 'I greet you, Watcher.'

'And I greet you, Gormon.'

'My name now is Victorious Thirteen.'

'I now am called Tomis of the Rememberers,' I said.

Manrule Seven remarked, 'When did you two become such fast friends?'

'In the time of the conquest,' said Victorious Thirteen. 'While performing my duties as an advance scout, I encountered this man in Talya and journed with him to Roum. But we were companions, in truth, and not friends.'

I trembled. 'Where is the Flier Avluela?'

'In Pars, I believe,' he said offhandedly. 'She spoke of returning to Hind, to the place of her people.'

'You loved her only a short while, then?'

'We were more companions than lovers,' said the invader. 'It was a passing thing for us.'

'For you, maybe,' I said.

'For us.'

'And for this passing thing you stole a man's eyes?'

He who had been Gormon shrugged. 'I did that to teach a proud creature a lesson in pride.'

'You said at the time that your motive was jealousy,' I reminded him. 'You claimed to act out of love.'

Victorious Thirteen appeared to lose interest in me. To Manrule Seven he said, 'Why is this man here? Why have you summoned me?'

'The Prince of Roum is in Perris,' said Manrule Seven. Victorious Thirteen registered sudden surprise.

Manrule Seven went on, 'He is a Prisoner of the Rememberers. This man offers a strange bargain. You know the Prince better than any of us; I ask your advice.'

The Procurator sketched the outlines of the situation. He who had been Gormon listened thoughtfully, saying nothing. At the end, Manrule Seven said, 'The problem is this: shall we give amnesty to a proscribed Dominator?'

'He is blind,' said Victorious Thirteen. 'His power is gone. His followers are scattered. His spirit may be unbroken, but he presents no danger to us. I say accept the bargain.'

'There are administrative risks in exempting a Dominator

from arrest,' Manrule Seven pointed out. 'Nevertheless, I agree. We undertake the deal.' To me he said, 'Tell us the location of the document we desire.'

'Arrange the liberation of the Prince of Roum first,' I said calmly.

Both invaders displayed amusement. 'Fair enough,' said Manrule Seven. 'But look: how can we be certain that you'll keep your word? Anything might happen to you in the next hour while we're freeing the Prince.'

'A suggestion,' put in Victorious Thirteen. 'This is not so much a matter of mutual mistrust as it is one of timing. Tomis, why not record the document's location on a six-hour delay cube? We'll prime the cube so that it will release its information only if within that six hours the Prince of Roum himself, and no one else, commands it to do so. If we haven't found and freed the Prince in that time, the cube will destruct. If we do release the Prince, the cube will give us the information, even if – ah – something should have happened to you in the interval.'

'You cover all contingencies,' I said.

'Are we agreed?' Manrule Seven asked.

'We are agreed,' I said.

They brought me a cube and placed me under a privacy screen while I inscribed on its glossy surface the rack number and sequence equations of the document I had discovered. Moments passed; the cube everted itself and the information vanished into its opaque depths. I offered it to them.

Thus did I betray my Earthborn heritage and perform a service for our conquerors, out of loyalty to a blinded wife-stealing Prince.

7

DAWN had come by this time. I did not accompany the invaders to the Hall of Rememberers; it was no business of mine to oversee the intricate events that must ensue, and I preferred to be elsewhere. A fine drizzle was falling as I turned down the gray streets that bordered the dark Senn. The timeless river, its surface stippled by the drops, swept unwearingly against stone arches of First Cycle antiquity, bridges spanning uncountable millennia, survivors from an era when the only problems of mankind were of his own making. Morning engulfed the city. Through an old and ineradicable reflex I searched for my instruments so that I could do my Watching, and had to remind myself that that was far behind me now. The Watchers were disbanded, the enemy had come, and old Wuellig, now Tomis of the Rememberers, had sold himself to mankind's foes.

In the shadow of a twin-steepled religious house of the ancient Christers I let myself be enticed into the booth of a Somnambulist. This guild is not one with which I have often had dealings; in my way I am wary of charlatans, and charlatans are abundant in our time. The Somnambulist, in a state of trance, claims to see what has been, what is, and what will be. I know something of trances myself, for as a Watcher I entered such a state four times each day; but a Watcher with pride in his craft much necessarily despise the tawdry ethics of those who use second sight for gain, as Somnambulists do.

However, while among the Rememberers I had learned, to my surprise, that Somnambulists frequently were consulted to aid in unearthing some site of ancient times, and that they had served the Rememberers well. Though still skeptical, I was willing to be instructed. And, at the moment, I needed a shelter from the storm that was breaking over the Hall of Rememberers.

A dainty, mincing figure garbed in black greeted me with a mocking bow as I entered the low-roofed booth.

'I am Samit of the Somnambulists,' he said in a high, whining voice. 'I offer you welcome and good tidings. Behold my companion, the Somnambulist Murta.'

The Somnambulist Murta was a robust woman in lacy robes. Her face was heavy with flesh, deep rings of darkness surrounded her eyes, a trace of mustache lined her upper lip. Somnambulists work their trade in teams, one to do the huckstering, one to perform; most teams were man and wife, as was this. My mind rebelled at the thought of the embrace of the flesh-mountain Murta and the miniature-man Samit, but it was no concern of mine. I took my seat as Samit indicated. On a table nearby I saw some food tablets of several colors; I had interrupted this family's breakfast. Murta, deep in trance, wandered the room with ponderous strides, now and again grazing some article of furniture in a gentle way. Some Somnambulists, it is said, waken only two or three hours of the twenty, simply to take meals and relieve bodily needs; there are some who ostensibly live in continuous trance and are fed and cared for by acolytes.

I scarcely listened as Samit of the Somnambulists delivered his sales-talk in rapid, feverish bursts of ritualized word-clusters. It was pitched to the ignorant; Somnambulists do much of their trade with Servitors and Clowns and other menials. At length, seemingly sensing my impatience, he cut short his extolling of the Somnambulist Murta's abilities and asked me what it was I wished to know.

'Surely the Somnambulist already is aware of that,' I said.

'You wish a general analysis?'

'I want to know of the fate of those about me. I wish particularly for the Somnambulist's concentration to center on events now occurring in the Hall of Rememberers.'

Samit tapped long fingernails against the smooth table and shot a glaring look at the cowlike Murta. 'Are you in contact with the truth?' he asked her.

Her reply was a long feathery sigh wrenched from the core of all the quivering meat of her.

'What do you see?' he asked her.

She began to mutter thickly. Somnambulists speak in a language not otherwise used by mankind; it is a harsh thing of edgy sounds, which some claim is descended from an

118

ancient tongue of Agupt. I know nothing of that. To me it sounded incoherent, fragmentary, impossible to hold meaning. Samit listened a while, then nodded in satisfaction and extended his palm to me.

'There is a great deal,' he said.

We discussed the fee, bargained briefly, came to a settlement. 'Go on,' I told him. 'Interpret the truth.'

Cautiously he began, 'There are outworlders involved in this, and also several members of the guild of Rememberers.' I was silent, giving him no encouragement. 'They are drawn together in a difficult quarrel. A man without eyes is at the heart of it.'

I sat upright with a jolt.

Samit smiled in cool triumph. 'The man without eyes has fallen from greatness. He is Earth, shall we say, broken by conquerors? Now he is near the end of his time. He seeks to restore his former condition, but he knows it is impossible. He has caused a Rememberer to violate an oath. To their guildhall have come several of the conquerors to – to chastise him? No. No. To free him from captivity. Shall I continue?'

'Quickly!'

'You have received all that you have paid for.'

I scowled. This was extortion; but yet the Somnambulist had clearly seen the truth. I had learned nothing here that I did not already know, but that was sufficient to tell me I might learn more. I added to my fee.

Samit closed his fist on my coins and conferred once more with Murta. She spoke at length, in some agitation, whirling several times, colliding violently with a musty divan.

Samit said, 'The man without eyes has come between a man and his wife. The outraged husband seeks punishment; the outworlders will thwart that. The outworlders seek hidden truths; they will find them, with a traitor's help. The man without eyes seeks freedom and power; he will find peace. The stained wife seeks amusement; she will find hardship.'

'And I?' I said into an obstinate and expensive silence. 'You say nothing of me!'

'You will leave Perris soon, in the same manner as you entered it. You will not leave alone. You will not leave in your present guild.'

119

What will be my destination?'

'You know that as well as we do, so why waste your money to tell you?'

He fell silent again.

'Tell me what will befall me as I journey to Jorslem,' I said.

'You could not afford such information. Futures become costly. I advise you to settle for what you now know.'

'I have some questions about what has already been said.'

'We do not clarify at any price.'

He grinned. I felt the force of his contempt. The Somnambulist Murta, still bumbling about the room, groaned and belched. The powers with whom she was in contact appeared to impart new information to her; she whimpered, shivered, made a blurred chuckling sound. Samit spoke to her in their language. She replied at length. He peered at me. 'At no cost,' he said, 'a final information. Your life is in no danger, but your spirit is. It would be well if you made your peace with the Will as quickly as possible. Recover your moral orientation. Remember your true loyalties. Atone for well-intentioned sins. I can say no more.'

Indeed Murta stirred and seemed to wake. Great slabs of flesh jiggled in her face and body as the convulsion of leaving the trance came over her. Her eyes opened, but I saw only whites, a terrible sight. Her thick lips twitched to reveal crumbling teeth. Samit beckoned me out with quick brushing gestures of his tiny hands. I fled into a dark, rain-drenched morning.

Hurriedly I returned to the Hall of Rememberers, arriving there out of breath, with a red spike of pain behind my breastbone. I paused a while outside the superb building to recover my strength. Floaters passed overhead, leaving the guildhall from an upper level. My courage nearly failed me. But in the end I entered the hall and ascended to the level of the suite of Elegro and Olmayne.

A knot of agitated Rememberers filled the hall. A buzz of whispered comment drifted toward me. I pressed forward; and a man whom I recognized as high in the councils of the guild held up a hand and said, 'What business do you have here, apprentice?'

'I am Tomis, who was sponsored by the Rememberer Olmayne. My chamber is close to here.'

'Tomis!' a voice cried.

I was seized and thrust ahead into the familiar suite, now a scene of devastation.

A dozen Rememberers stood about, fingering their shawls in distress. I recognized among them the taut and elegant figure of Chancellor Kenishal, his gray eyes now dull with despair. Beneath a coverlet to the left of the entrance lay a crumpled figure in the robes of a Pilgrim: the Prince of Roum, dead in his own pooled blood. His gleaming mask, now stained, lay beside him. At the opposite side of the room, slumped against an ornate credenza containing Second Cycle artifacts of great beauty, was the Rememberer Elegro, seemingly asleep, looking furious and surprised both at once. His throat was transfixed by a single slender dart. To the rear, with burly Rememberers flanking her, stood the Rememberer Olmayne looking wild and disheveled. Her scarlet robe was torn in front and revealed high white breasts; her black hair tumbled in disorder; her satiny skin glistened with perpiration. She appeared lost in a dream, far from these present surroundings.

'What has happened here?' I asked.

'Murder twice over,' said Chancellor Kenishal in a broken voice. He advanced toward me: a tall, haggard man, white-haired, an uncontrollable tic working in the lid of one eye. 'When did you last see these people alive, apprentice?'

'In the night.'

'How did you come to be here?'

'A visit, no more.'

'Was there a disturbance?'

'A quarrel between the Rememberer Elegro and the Pilgrim, yes,' I admitted.

'Over what?' asked the Chancellor thinly.

I looked uneasily at Olmayne, but she saw nothing and heard less.

'Over her,' I said.

I heard snickerings from the other Rememberers. They nudged each other, nodded, even smiled; I had confirmed the scandal. The Chancellor grew more solemn.

He indicated the body of the Prince.

'This was your companion when you entered Perris,' he said. 'Did you know of his true identity?'

I moistened my lips. 'I had suspicions.'

121

'That he was—'

'The fugitive Prince of Roum,' I said. I did not dare attempt subterfuges now; my status was precarious.

More nods, more nudges. Chancellor Kenishal said, 'This man was subject to arrest. It was not your place to conceal your knowledge of his identity.'

I remained mute.

The Chancellor went on, 'You have been absent from this hall for some hours. Tell us of your activities after leaving the suite of Elegro and Olmayne.'

'I called upon the Procurator Manrule Seven,' I said.

Sensation.

'For what purpose?'

'To inform the Procurator,' I said, 'that the Prince of Roum had been apprehended and was now in the suite of a Rememberer. I did this at the instruction of the Rememberer Elegro. After delivering my information I walked the streets several hours for no particular end, and returned here to find – to find—'

'To find everything in chaos,' said Chancellor Kenishal. 'The Procurator was here at dawn. He visited this suite; both Elegro and the Prince must still have been alive at that time. Then he went into our archives and removed – and removed – material of the highest sensitivity – the highest sensitivity – removed – material not believed to be accessible to – the highest sensitivity—' The Chancellor faltered. Like some intricate machine smitten with instant rust, he slowed his motions, emitted rasping sounds, appeared to be on the verge of systematic breakdown. Several high Rememberers rushed to his aid; one thrust a drug against his arm. In moments the Chancellor appeared to recover. 'These murders occurred after the Procurator departed from the building,' he said. 'The Rememberer Olmayne has been unable to give us information concerning them. Perhaps you, apprentice, know something of value.'

'I was not present. Two Somnambulists near the Senn will testify that I was with them at the time the crimes were committed.'

Someone guffawed at my mention of Somnambulists. Let them; I was not seeking to retrieve dignity at a time like this. I knew that I was in peril.

The Chancellor said slowly, 'You will go to your chamber,

122

apprentice, and you will remain there to await full interrogation. Afterwards you will leave the building and be gone from Perris within twenty hours. By virtue of my authority I declare you expelled from the guild of Rememberers.'

Forewarned as I had been by Samit, I was nevertheless stunned.

'*Expelled?* Why?'

'We can no longer trust you. Too many mysteries surround you. You bring us a Prince and conceal your suspicions; you are present at murderous quarrels; you visit a Procurator in the middle of the night. You may even have helped to bring about the calamitous loss suffered by our archive this morning. We have no desire for men of enigmas here. We sever our relationship with you.' The Chancellor waved his hand in a grand sweep. 'To your chamber now, to await interrogation, and then go!'

I was rushed from the room. As the entrance pit closed behind me, I looked back and saw the Chancellor, his face ashen, topple into the arms of his associates, while in the same instant the Rememberer Olmayne broke from her freeze and fell to the floor, screaming.

8

ALONE in my chamber, I spent a long while gathering together my possessions, though I owned little. The morning was well along before a Rememberer whom I did not know came to me; he carried interrogation equipment. I eyed it uneasily, thinking that all would be up with me if the Rememberers found proof that it was I who had betrayed the location of that compound record to the invaders. Already they suspected me of it; the Chancellor had hesitated to make the accusation only because it must have seemed odd to him that an apprentice such as myself would have cared to make a private search of the guild archive.

Fortune rode with me. My interrogator was concerned only with the details of the slaying; and once he had determined that I knew nothing on that subject, he let me be, warning me to depart from the hall within the allotted time. I told him I would do so.

But first I needed rest. I had had none that night; and so I drank a three-hour draught and settled into soothing sleep. When I awakened a figure stood beside me: the Rememberer Olmayne.

She appeared to have aged greatly since the previous evening. She was dressed in a single chaste tunic of a sombre color, and she wore neither ornament nor decoration. Her features were rigidly set. I mastered my surprise at finding her there, and sat up, mumbling an apology for my delay in acknowledging her presence.

'Be at ease,' she said gently. 'Have I broken your sleep?'

'I had my full hours.'

'I have had none. But there will be time for sleep later. We owe each other explanations, Tomis.'

'Yes.' I rose uncertainly. 'Are you well? I saw you earlier, and you seemed lost in trance.'

'They have given me medicines,' she replied.

'Tell me what you can about last night.'

Her eyelids slid momentarily closed. 'You were there when

124

Elegro challenged us and was cast out by the Prince. Some hours later, Elegro returned. With him were the Procurator of Perris and several other invaders. Elegro appeared to be in a mood of great jubiliation. The Procurator produced a cube and commanded the Prince to put his hand to it. The Prince balked, but Manrule Seven persuaded him finally to cooperate. When he had touched the cube, the Procurator and Elegro departed, leaving the Prince and myself together again, neither of us comprehending what had happened. Guards were posted to prevent the Prince from leaving. Not long afterward the Procurator and Elegro returned. Now Elegro seemed subdued and even confused, while the Procurator was clearly exhilarated. In our room the Procurator announced that amnesty had been granted to the former Prince of Roum, and that no man was to harm him. Thereupon all of the invaders departed.'

'Proceed.'

Olmayne spoke as though a Somnambulist. 'Elegro did not appear to comprehend what had occurred. He cried out that treason had been done; he screamed that he had been betrayed. An angry scene followed. Elegro was womanish in his fury; the Prince grew more haughty; each ordered the other to leave the suite. The quarrel became so violent that the carpet itself began to die. The petals drooped; the little mouths gaped. The climax came swiftly. Elegro seized a weapon and threatened to use it if the Prince did not leave at once. The Prince misjudged Elegro's temper, thought he was bluffing, and came forward as if to throw Elegro out. Elegro slew the Prince. An instant later I grasped a dart from our rack of artifacts and hurled it into Elegro's throat. The dart bore poison; he died at once. I summoned others, and I remember no more.'

'A strange night,' I said.

'Too strange. Tell me now, Tomis: why did the Procurator come, and why did he not take the Prince into custody?'

I said, 'The Procurator came because I asked him to, under the orders of your late husband. The Procurator did not arrest the Prince because the Prince's liberty had been purchased.'

'At what price?'

'The price of a man's shame,' I said.

'You speak a riddle.'

'The truth dishonors me. I beg you not to press me for it.'

'The Chancellor spoke of a document that had been taken by the Procurator—'

'It has to do with that,' I confessed, and Olmayne looked toward the floor and asked no further questions.

I said ultimately, 'You have committed a murder, then. What will your punishment be?'

'The crime was committed in passion and fear,' she replied. 'There will be no penalty of the civil administration. But I am expelled from my guild for my adultery and my act of violence.'

'I offer my regrets.'

'And I am commanded to undertake the Pilgrimage to Jorslem to purify my soul. I must leave within the day, or my life is forfeit to the guild.'

'I too am expelled,' I told her. 'And I too am bound at last for Jorslem, though of my own choosing.'

'May we travel together?'

My hesitation betrayed me. I had journeyed here with a blind Prince; I cared very little to depart with a murderous and guildless woman. Perhaps the time had come to travel alone. Yet the Somnambulist had said I would have a companion.

Olmayne said smoothly, 'You lack enthusiasm. Perhaps I can create some in you.' She opened her tunic. I saw mounted between the snowy hills of her breasts a gray pouch. She was tempting me not with her flesh but with an overpocket. 'In this,' she said, 'is all that the Prince of Roum carried in his thigh. He showed me those treasures, and I removed them from his body as he lay dead in my room. Also there are certain objects of my own. I am not without resources. We will travel comfortably. Well?'

'I find it hard to refuse.'

'Be ready in two hours.'

'I am ready now,' I said.

'Wait, then.'

She left me to myself. Nearly two hours later she returned, clad now in the mask and robes of a Pilgrim. Over her arm she held a second set of Pilgrim's gear, which she offered to me. Yes: I was guildless now, and it was an un-

126

safe way to travel. I would go, then, as a Pilgrim to Jorslem. I donned the unfamiliar gear. We gathered our possessions.

'I have notified the guild of Pilgrims,' she declared as we left the Hall of Rememberers. 'We are fully registered. Later today we may hope to receive our starstones. How does the mask feel, Tomis?'

'Snug.'

'As it should be.'

Our route out of Perris took us across the great plaza before the ancient gray holy building of the old creed. A crowd had gathered; I saw invaders at the center of the group. Beggars made the profitable orbit about it. They ignored us, for no one begs from a Pilgrim; but I collared one rascal with a gouged face and said, 'What ceremony is taking place here?'

'Funeral of the Prince of Roum,' he said. 'By order of the Procurator. State funeral with all the trimmings. They're making a real festival out of it.'

'Why hold such an event in Perris?' I asked. 'How did the Prince die?'

'Look, ask somebody else. I got work to do.'

He wriggled free and scrambled on to work the crowd.

'Shall we attend the funeral?' I asked Olmayne.

'Best not to.'

'As you wish.'

We moved toward the massive stone bridge that spanned the Senn. Behind us, a brilliant blue glow arose as the pyre of the dead Prince was kindled. That pyre lit the way for us as we made our slow way through the night, eastward to Jorslem.

127

PART III

THE ROAD TO JORSLEM

1

OUR WORLD was now truly theirs. All the way across
Eyrop I could see that the invaders had taken everything,
and we belonged to them as beasts in a barnyard belong
to the farmer.

They were everywhere, like fleshy weeds taking root
after a strange storm. They walked with cool confidence, as
if telling us by the sleekness of their movements that the
Will had withdrawn favor from us and conferred it upon
them. They were not cruel to us, and yet they drained us
of vitality by their mere presence among us. Our sun, our
moons, our museums of ancient relics, our ruins of former
cycles, our cities, our palaces, our future, our present, and
our past had all undergone a transfer of title. Our lives now
lacked meaning.

At night the blaze of the stars mocked us. All the universe looked down on our shame.

The cold wind of winter told us that for our sins our
freedom had been lost. The bright heat of summer told us
that for our pride we had been humbled.

Through a changed world we moved, stripped of our
past selves. I, who had roved the stars each day now had
lost that pleasure. Now, bound for Jorslem, I found cool
comfort in the hope that as a Pilgrim I might gain redemption and renewal in that holy city. Olmayne and I repeated
each night the rituals of our Pilgrimage toward that end:

'We yield to the Will.'
'We yield to the Will.'
'In all things great and small.'
'In all things great and small.'
'And ask forgiveness.'
'And ask forgiveness.'

'For sins actual and potential.'
'For sins actual and potential.'
'And pray for understanding and repose.'
'And pray for understanding and repose.'
'Through all our days until redemption comes.'
'Through all our days until redemption comes.'

Thus we spoke the words. Saying them, we clutched the cool polished spheres of starstone, icy as frostflowers, and made communion with the Will. And so we journeyed Jorslemward in this world that no longer was owned by man.

2

It was at the Talyan approach to Land Bridge that Olmayne first used her cruelty on me. Olmayne was cruel by first nature; I had had ample proof of that in Perris; and yet we had been Pilgrims together for many months, traveling from Perris eastward over the mountains and down the length of Talya to the Bridge, and she had kept her claws sheathed. Until this place.

The occasion was our halting by a company of invaders coming north from Afreek. There were perhaps twenty of them, tall and harsh-faced, proud of being masters of conquered Earth. They rode in a gleaming covered vehicle of their own manufacture, long and narrow, with thick sand-colored treads and small windows. We could see the vehicle from far away, raising a cloud of dust as it neared us.

This was a hot time of year. The sky itself was the color of sand, and it was streaked with folded sheets of heat-radiation – glowing and terrible energy streams of turquoise and gold.

Perhaps fifty of us stood beside the road, with the land of Talya at our backs and the continent of Afreek before us. We were a varied group: some Pilgrims, like Olmayne and myself, making the trek toward the holy city of Jorslem, but also a random mix of the rootless, men and women who floated from continent to continent for lack of other purpose. I counted in the band five former Watchers, and also several Indexers, a Sentinel, a pair of Communicants, a Scribe, and even a few Changelings. We gathered into a straggling assembly awarding the road by default to the invaders.

Land Bridge is not wide, and the road will not allow many to use it at any time. Yet in normal times the flow of traffic had always gone in both directions at once. Here, today, we feared to go forward while invaders were this close, and so we remained clustered timidly, watching our conquerors approach.

One of the Changelings detached himself from the others of his kind and moved toward me. He was small of stature for that breed, but wide through the shoulders; his skin seemed much too tight for his frame; his eyes were large and green-rimmed; his hair grew in thick widely spaced pedestal-like clumps, and his nose was barely perceptible, so that his nostrils appeared to sprout from his upper lip. Despite this he was less grotesque than most Changelings appear. His expression was solemn, but had a hint of bizarre playfulness lurking somewhere.

He said in a voice that was little more than a feathery whisper. 'Do you think we'll be delayed long, Pilgrims?'

In former times one did not address a Pilgrim unsolicited – especially if one happened to be a Changeling. Such customs meant nothing to me, but Olmayne drew back with a hiss of distaste.

I said, 'We will wait here until our masters allow us to pass. Is there any choice?'

'None, friend, none.'

At that *friend*, Olmayne hissed again and glowered at the little Changeling. He turned to her, and his anger showed, for suddenly six parallel bands of scarlet pigment blazed brightly beneath the glossy skin of his cheeks. But his only overt response to her was a courteous bow. He said, 'I introduce myself. I am Bernalt, naturally guildless, a native of Nayrub in Deeper Afreek. I do not inquire after your names, Pilgrims. Are you bound for Jorslem?'

'Yes,' I said, as Olmayne swung about to present her back. 'And you? Home to Nayrub after travels?'

'No,' said Bernalt. 'I go to Jorslem also.'

Instantly I felt cold and hostile, my initial response to the Changeling's suave charm fading at once. I had had a Changeling, false though he turned out to be, as a traveling companion before; he too had been charming, but I wanted no more like him. Edgily, distantly, I said, 'May I ask what business a Changeling might have in Jorslem?'

He detected the chill in my tone, and his huge eyes registered sorrow. 'We too are permitted to visit the holy city, I remind you. Even our kind. Do you fear that Changelings will once again seize the shrine of renewal, as we did a thousand years ago before we were cast down into guildlessness?' He laughed harshly. 'I threaten no one,

Pilgrim. I am hideous of face, but not dangerous. May the Will grant you what you seek, Pilgrim.' He made a gesture of respect and went back to the other Changelings.

Furious, Olmayne spun round on me.

'Why do you talk to such beastly creatures?'

'The man approached me. He was merely being friendly. We are all cast together here, Olmayne, and—'

'*Man. Man!* You call a Changeling a man?'

'They *are* human, Olmayne.'

'Just barely. Tomis, I loathe such monsters. My flesh creeps to have them near me. If I could, I'd banish them from this world!'

'Where is the serene tolerance a Rememberer must cultivate?'

She flamed at the mockery in my voice. 'We are not required to love Changelings, Tomis. They are one of the curses laid upon our planet – parodies of humanity, enemies of truth and beauty. I despise them!'

It was not a unique attitude. But I had no time to reproach Olmayne for her intolerance; the vehicle of the invaders was drawing near. I hoped we might resume our journey once it went by. It slowed and halted, however, and several of the invaders came out. They walked unhurriedly toward us, their long arms dangling like slack ropes.

'Who is the leader here?' asked one of them.

No one replied, for we were independent of one another in our travel.

The invader said impatiently, after a moment, 'No leader? No leader? Very well, all of you, listen. The road must be cleared. A convoy is coming through. Go back to Palerm and wait until tomorrow.'

'But I must be in Agupt by—' the Scribe began.

'Land Bridge is closed today,' said the invader. 'Go back to Palerm.'

His voice was calm. The invaders are never peremptory, never overbearing. They have the poise and assurance of those who are secure possessors.

The Scribe shivered, his jowls swinging, and said no more.

Several of the others by the side of the road looked as if they wished to protest. The Sentinel turned away and

133

spat. A man who boldly wore the mark of the shattered guild of Defenders in his cheek clenched his fists and plainly fought back a surge of fury. The Changelings whispered to one another. Bernalt smiled bitterly at me and shrugged.

Go back to Palerm? Waste a day's march in this heat? For what? For what?

The invader gestured casually, telling us to disperse.

Now it was that Olmayne was unkind to me. In a low voice she said, 'Explain to them, Tomis, that you are in the pay of the Procurator of Perris, and they will let the two of us pass.'

Her dark eyes glittered with mockery and contempt.

My shoulders sagged as if she had loaded ten years on me. 'Why did you say such a thing?' I asked.

'It's hot. I'm tired. It's idiotic of them to send us back to Palerm.'

'I agree. But I can do nothing. Why do you hurt me?'

'Does the truth hurt that much?'

'I am no collaborator, Olmayne.'

She laughed. 'You say that so well! But you are, Tomis, you are! You sold them the documents.'

'To save the Prince, your lover,' I reminded her.

'You dealt with the invaders, though. No matter what your motive was, that fact remains.'

'Stop it, Olmayne.'

'Now you give me orders?'

'Olmayne—'

'Go up to them, Tomis. Tell them who you are, make them let us go ahead.'

'The convoys would run us down on the road. In any case I have no influence with invaders. I am not the Procurator's man.'

'I'll die before I go back to Palerm!'

'Die, then,' I said wearily, and turned my back on her.

'Traitor! Treacherous old fool! Coward!'

I pretended to ignore her, but I felt the fire of her words. There was no falsehood in them, only malice. I *had* dealt with the conquerors, I *had* betrayed the guild that sheltered me, I *had* violated the code that calls for sullen passivity as our only way of protest for Earth's defeat. All true; yet it was unfair for her to reproach me with it. I had given no thought to higher matters of patriotism when

134

I broke my trust; I was trying only to save a man to whom I felt bound, a man moreover with whom she was in love. It was loathsome of Olmayne to tax me with treason now, to torment my conscience, merely because of a petty rage at the heat and dust of the road.

But this woman had coldly slain her own husband. Why should she not be malicious in trifles as well?

The invaders had their way; we abandoned the road and straggled back to Palerm, a dismal, sizzling, sleepy town. That evening, as if to console us, five Fliers passing in formation overhead took a fancy to the town, and in the moonless night they came again and again through the sky, three men and two women, ghostly and slender and beautiful. I stood watching them for more than an hour, until my soul itself seemed lifted from me and into the air to join them. Their great shimmering wings scarcely hid the starlight; their pale angular bodies moved in graceful arcs, arms held pressed close to sides, legs together, backs gently curved. The sight of these five stirred my memories of Avluela and left me tingling with troublesome emotions.

The Fliers made their last pass and were gone. The false moons entered the sky soon afterward. I went into our hostelry then, and shortly Olmayne asked admittance to my room.

She looked contrite. She carried a squat octagonal flask of green wine, not a Talyan brew but something from an outworld, no doubt purchased at great price.

'Will you forgive me, Tomis?' she asked. 'Here. I know you like these wines.'

'I would rather not have had those words before, and not have the wine now,' I told her.

'My temper grows short in the heat. I'm sorry, Tomis. I said a stupid and tactless thing.'

I forgave her, in hope of a smoother journey thereafter, and we drank most of the wine, and then she went to her own room nearby to sleep. Pilgrims must live chaste lives – not that Olmayne would ever have bedded with such a withered old fossil as I, but the commandments of our adopted guild prevented the question from arising.

For a long while I lay awake beneath a lash of guilt. In her impatience and wrath Olmayne had stung me at my

135

vulnerable place: I was a betrayer of mankind. I wrestled with the issue almost to dawn.

– What had I done?

I had revealed to our conquerors a certain document.

– Did the invaders have a moral right to the document?

It told of the shameful treatment they had had at the hands of our ancestors.

– What, then, was wrong about giving it to them?

One does not aid one's conquerors even when they are morally superior to one.

– Is a small treason a serious thing?

There are no small treasons.

– Perhaps the complexity of the matter should be investigated. I did not act out of love of the enemy, but to aid a friend.

Nevertheless I collaborated with our foes.

–This obstinate self-laceration smacks of sinful pride.

But I feel my guilt. I drown in shame.

In this unprofitable way I consumed the night. When the day brightened, I rose and looked skyward and begged the Will to help me find redemption in the waters of the house of renewal in Jorslem, at the end of my Pilgrimage. Then I went to awaken Olmayne.

3

LAND BRIDGE was open on this day, and we joined the
throng that was crossing over out of Talya into Afreek. It
was the second time I had traveled Land Bridge, for the
year before – it seemed so much farther in the past – I had
come the other way, out of Agupt and bound for Roum.

There are two main routes for Pilgrims from Eyrop to
Jorslem. The northern route involves going through the
Dark Lands east of Talya, taking the ferry at Stanbool, and
skirting the western coast of the continent of Ais to Jorslem.
It was the route I would have preferred since, of all the
world's great cities, old Stanbol is the one I have never
visited. But Olmayne had been there to do research in the
days when she was a Rememberer, and disliked the place;
and so we took the southern route – across Land Bridge
into Afreek and along the shore of the great Lake Medit,
through Agupt and the fringes of the Arban Desert and up
to Jorslem.

A true Pilgrim travels only by foot. It was not an idea
that had much appeal to Olmayne, and though we walked
a great deal, we rode whenever we could. She was shameless in commandeering transportation. On only the second
day of our journey she had gotten us a ride from a rich
Merchant bound for the coast; the man had no intention
of sharing his sumptuous vehicle with anyone, but he could
not resist the sensuality of Olmayne's deep, musical voice,
even though it issued from the sexless grillwork of a Pilgrim's mask.

The Merchant traveled in style. For him the conquest
of Earth might never have happened, nor even all the long
centuries of Third Cycle decline. His self-primed landcar
was four times the length of a man and wide enough to
house five people in comfort; and it shielded its riders
against the outer world as effectively as a womb. There was
no direct vision, only a series of screens revealing upon
command what lay outside. The temperature never varied

from a chosen norm. Spigots supplied liquers and stronger things; food tablets were available; pressure couches insulated travelers against the irregularities of the road. For illumination, there was slavelight keyed to the Merchant's whims. Beside the main couch sat a thinking cap, but I never learned whether the Merchant carried a pickled brain for his private use in the depths of the landcar, or enjoyed some sort of remote contact with the memory tanks of the cities through which he passed.

He was a man of pomp and bulk, clearly a savourer of his own flesh. Deep olive skin, with a thick pompadour of well-oiled black hair and somber, scrutinizing eyes, he rejoiced in his solidity and in his control of an uncertain environment. He dealt, we learned, in foodstuffs of other worlds; he bartered our poor manufacturers for the delicacies of the starborn ones. Now he was en route to Marsay to examine a cargo of hallucinatory insects newly come in from one of the Belt planets.

'You like the car?' he asked, seeing our awe. Olmayne, no stranger to ease herself, was peering at the dense inner mantle of diamonded brocade in obvious amazement. 'It was owned by the Comt of Perris,' he went on. 'Yes, I mean it, the Comt himself. They turned his palace into a museum, you know.'

'I know,' Olmayne said softly.

'This was his chariot. It was supposed to be part of the museum, but I bought it off a crooked invader. You didn't know they had crooked ones too, eh?' The Merchant's robust laughter caused the sensitive mantle on the walls of the car to recoil in disdain. 'This one was the Procurator's boy friend. Yes, they've got *those*, too. He was looking for a certain fancy root that grows on a planet of the Fishes, something to give his virility a little boost, you know, and he learned that I controlled the whole supply here, and so we were able to work out a little deal. Of course, I had to have the car adapted, a little. The Comt kept four neuters up front and powered the engine right off their metabolisms, you understand, running the thing on thermal differentials. Well, that's a fine way to power a car, if you're a Comt, but it uses up a lot of neuters through the year, and I felt I'd be overreaching my status if I tried anything like that. It might get me into trouble with the invaders, too. So I had the drive compartment stripped down and replaced with a standard heavy-duty roller-wagon engine – a really subtle job – and there you are. You're lucky to be in here. It's only that you're Pilgrims. Ordinarily I don't let folks come inside, on account of them feeling envy, and envious folks are dangerous to a man who's made something out of his life. Yet the Will brought you two to me. Heading for Jorslem, eh?'

'Yes,' Olmayne said.

'Me too, but not yet! Not just yet, thank you!' He patted his middle. 'I'll be there, you can bet on it, when I feel ready for renewal, but that's a good way off, the Will willing! You two been Pilgriming long?'

'No,' Olmayne said.

'A lot of folks went Pilgriming after the conquest, I guess. Well, I don't blame 'em. We each adapt in our own ways to changing times. Say, you carrying those little stones the Pilgrims carry?'

'Yes,' Olmayne said.

'Mind if I see one? Always been fascinated by the things. There was this trader from one of the Darkstar worlds – little skinny bastard with skin like oozing tar – he offered me ten quintals of the things. Said they were genuine, gave you the real communion, just like the Pilgrims had. I told him no, I wasn't going to fool with the Will. Some things you don't do, even for profit. But afterward I wished I'd kept one as a souvenir. I never even touched one.' He stretched a hand toward Olmayne. 'Can I see?'

'We may not let others handle the starstone,' I said.

'I wouldn't tell anybody you let me!'

'It is forbidden.'

'Look, it's private in here, the most private place on Earth, and—'

'Please. What you ask is impossible.'

His face darkened, and I thought for a moment he would halt the car and order us out, which would have caused me no grief. My hand slipped into my pouch to finger the frigid starstone sphere that I had been given at the outset of my Pilgrimage. The touch of my fingertips brought faint resonances of the communion-trance to me, and I shivered in pleasure. He must not have it, I swore. But the crisis

139

passed without incident. The Merchant, having tested us and found resistance, did not choose to press the matter.

We sped onward toward Marsay.

He was not a likeable man, but he had a certain gross charm, and we were rarely offended by his words. Olmayne, who after all was a fastidious woman and had lived most of her years in the glossy seclusion of the Hall of Rememberers, found him harder to take than I; my intolerances have been well blunted by a lifetime of wandering. But even Olmayne seemed to find him amusing when he boasted of his wealth and influence, when he told of the women who waited for him on many worlds, when he catalogued his homes and his trophies and the guildmasters who sought his counsel, when he bragged of friendships with former Masters and Dominators. He talked almost wholly of himself and rarely of us, for which we were thankful; once he asked how it was that a male Pilgrim and a female Pilgrim were traveling together, implying that we must be lovers; we admitted that the arrangement was slightly irregular and went on to another theme, and I think he remained persuaded of our unchastity. His bawdy guesses mattered not at all to me nor, I believe, to Olmayne. We had more serious guilts as our burdens.

Our Merchant's life seemed enviably undisrupted by the fall of our planet: he was as rich as ever, as comfortable, as free to move about. But even he felt occasionally irked by the presence of the invaders, as we found out by night not far from Marsay, when we were stopped at a checkpoint on the road.

Spy-eye scanners saw us coming, gave a signal to the spinnerets, and a golden spiderweb spurted into being from one shoulder of the highway to the other. The landcar's sensors detected it and instantly signaled us to a halt. The screens showed a dozen pale human faces clustered outside.

'Bandits?' Olmayne asked.

'Worse,' said the Merchant. 'Traitors.' He scowled and turned to his communicator horn. 'What is it?' he demanded.

'Get out for inspection.'

'By whose writ?'

'The Procurator of Marsay,' came the reply.

It was an ugly thing to behold: human beings acting as

140

road-agents for the invaders. But it was inevitable that we should have begun to drift into their civil service, since work was scarce, especially for those who had been in the defensive guilds. The Merchant began the complicated process of unsealing his car. He was stormy-faced with rage, but he was stymied, unable to pass the checkpoint's web. 'I go armed,' he whispered to us. 'Wait inside and fear nothing.'

He got out and engaged in a lengthy discussion, of which we could hear nothing, with the highway guards. At length some impasse must have forced recourse to higher authority, for three invaders abruptly appeared, waved their hired collaborators away, and surrounded the Merchant. His demeanor changed; his face grew oily and sly, his hands moved rapidly in eloquent gestures, his eyes glistened. He led the three interrogators to the car, opened it, and showed them his two passengers, ourselves. The invaders appeared puzzled by the sight of Pilgrims amid such opulence, but they did not ask us to step out. After some further conversation the Merchant rejoined us and sealed the car; the web was dissolved; we sped onward toward Marsay.

As we gained velocity he muttered curses and said, 'Do you know how I'd handle that long-armed filth? All we need is a coordinated plan. A night of knives: every ten Earthmen make themselves responsible for taking out one invader. We'd get them all.'

'Why has no one organized such a movement?' I asked.

'It's the job of the Defenders, and half of them are dead, and the other half's in the pay of *them*. It's not my place to set up a resistance movement. But that's how it should be done. Guerrilla action: sneak up behind 'em, give 'em the knife. Quick. Good old First Cycle methods; they've never lost their value.'

'More invaders would come,' Olmayne said morosely.

'Treat 'em the same way!'

'They would retaliate with fire. They would destroy our world,' she said.

'These invaders pretend to be civilized, more civilized than ourselves,' the Merchant replied. 'Such barbarity would give them a bad name on a million worlds. No, they wouldn't come with fire. They'd just get tired of having to

141

conquer us over and over, of losing so many men. And they'd go away, and we'd be free again.'

'Without having won redemption for our ancient sins,' I said.

'What's that, old man? What's that?'

'Never mind.'

'I suppose you wouldn't join them, either of you, if we struck back at them?'

I said, 'In former life I was a Watcher, and I devoted myself to the protection of this planet against them. I am no more fond of our masters than you are, and no less eager to see them depart. But your plan is not only impractical: it is also morally valueless. Mere bloody resistance would thwart the scheme the Will has devised for us. We must earn our freedom in a nobler way. We were not given this ordeal simply so that we might have practice in slitting throats.'

He looked at me with contempt and snorted. 'I should have remembered. I'm talking to Pilgrims. All right. Forget it all. I wasn't serious, anyway. Maybe you like the world the way it is, for all I know.'

'I do not,' I said.

He glanced at Olmayne. So did I, for I half-expected her to tell the Merchant that I had already done my bit of collaborating with our conquerors. But Olmayne fortunately was silent on that topic, as she would be for some months more, until that unhappy day by the approach to Land Bridge when, in her impatience, she taunted me with my sole fall from grace.

We left our benefactor in Marsay, spent the night in a Pilgrim hostelry, and set out on foot along the coast the next morning. And so we traveled, Olmayne and I, through pleasant lands swarming with invaders; now we walked, now we rode some peasant's rollerwagon, once even we were the guests of touring conquerors. We gave Roum a wide berth when we entered Talya, and turned south. And so we came to Land Bridge, and met delay, and had our frosty moment of bickering, and then were permitted to go on across that narrow tongue of sandy ground that links the lake-sundered continents. And so we crossed into Afreek, at last.

142

4

Our first night on the other side, after our long and dusty crossing, we tumbled into a grimy inn near the lake's edge. It was a square whitewashed stone building, practically windowless and arranged around a cool inner courtyard. Most of its clientele appeared to be Pilgrims, but there were some members of other guilds, chiefly Vendors and Transporters. At a room near the turning of the building there stayed a Rememberer, whom Olmayne avoided even though she did not know him; she simply did not wish to be reminded of her former guild.

Among those who took lodging there was the Changeling Bernalt. Under the new laws of the invaders, Changelings might stay at any public inn, not merely those set aside for their special use; yet it seemed a little strange to see him here. We passed in the corridor. Bernalt gave me a tentative smile, as though about to speak again, but the smile died and the glow left his eyes. He appeared to realize I was not ready to accept his friendship. Or perhaps he merely recalled that Pilgrims, by the laws of their guild, were not supposed to have much to do with guildless ones. That law still stood.

Olmayne and I had a greasy meal of soups and stews. Afterward I saw her to her room and began to wish her good night when she said, 'Wait. We'll do our communion together.'

'I've been seen coming into your room,' I pointed out. 'There will be whispering if I stay long.'

'We'll go to yours, then!'

Olmayne peered into the hall. All clear: she seized my wrist, and we rushed toward my chamber, across the way. Closing and sealing the warped door, she said, 'Your starstone, now!'

I took the stone from its hiding place in my robe, and she produced hers, and our hands closed upon them.

During this time of Pilgrimage I had found the starstone

a great comfort. Many seasons now had passed since I had last entered a Watcher's trance, but I was not yet reconciled entirely to the breaking of my old habit; the starstone provided a kind of substitute for the swooping ecstasy I had known in Watching.

Starstones come from one of the outer worlds – I could not tell you which — and may be had only by application to the guild. The stone itself determines whether one may be a Pilgrim, for it will burn the hand of one whom it considers unworthy to don the robe. They say that without exception every person who has enrolled in the guild of Pilgrims has shown uneasiness as the stone was offered to him for the first time.

'When they gave you yours,' Olmayne asked, 'were you worried?'

'Of course.'

'So was I.'

We waited for the stones to overwhelm us. I gripped mine tightly. Dark, shining, more smooth than glass, it glowed in my grasp like a pellet of ice, and I felt myself becoming attuned to the power of the Will.

First came a heightened perception of my surroundings. Every crack in the walls of this ancient inn seemed now a valley. The soft wail of the wind outside rose to a keen pitch. In the dim glow of the room's lamp I saw colors beyond the spectrum.

The quality of the experience the starstone offered was altogether different from that given by my instruments of Watching. That, too, was a transcending of self. When in a state of Watchfulness I was capable of leaving my Earth-bound identity and soaring at infinite speed over infinite range, perceiving all, and this is as close to godhood as a man is likely to come. The starstone provided none of the highly specific data that a Watcher's trance yielded. In the full spell I could see nothing, nor could I identify my surroundings. I knew only that when I let myself be drawn into the stone's effect, I was engulfed by something far larger than myself, that I was in direct contact with the matrix of the universe.

Call it communion with the Will.

From a great distance I heard Olmayne say, 'Do you

believe what some people say of these stones? That there is no communion, that it's all an electrical deception?'

'I have no theory about that,' I said. 'I am less interested in causes than in effects.'

Skeptics say that the starstones are nothing more than amplifying loops which bounce a man's own brain-waves back into his mind; the awesome oceanic entity with which one comes in contact, these scoffers hold, is merely the thunderous recycling oscillation of a single shuttling electrical pulse beneath the roof of the Pilgrim's own skull. Perhaps.

Olmayne extended the hand that gripped her stone. She said, 'When you were among the Rememberers, Tomis, did you study the history of early religion? All through time, man has sought union with the infinite. Many religions – not all! – have held forth the hope of such a divine merging.'

'And there were drugs, too,' I murmured.

'Certain drugs, yes, cherished for their ability to bring the taker momentarily to a sensation of oneness with the universe. These starstones, Tomis, are only the latest in a long sequence of devices for overcoming the greatest of human curses, that, is, the confinement of each individual soul within a single body. Our terrible isolation from one another and from the Will itself is more than most races of the universe would be able to bear. It seems unique to humanity.'

Her voice grew feathery and vague. She said much more, speaking to me out of the wisdom she had learned with the Rememberers, but her meaning eluded me; I was always quicker to enter communion than she, because of my training as a Watcher, and often her final words did not register.

That night as on other nights I seized my stone and felt the chill and closed my eyes, and heard the distant tolling of a mighty gong, the lapping of waves on an unknown beach, the whisper of the wind in an alien forest. And felt a summons. And yielded. And entered the state of communion. And gave myself up to the Will.

And slipped down through the layers of my life, through my youth and middle years, my wanderings, my old loves, my torments, my joys, my troubled later years, my treasons, my insufficiencies, my griefs, my imperfections.

And freed myself of myself. And shed my selfness. And merged. And became one of thousands of Pilgrims, not merely Olmayne nearby, but others trekking the mountains of Hind and the sands of Arba, Pilgrims at their devotions in Ais and Palash and Strayla, Pilgrims moving toward Jorslem on the journey that some complete in months, some in years, and some never at all. And shared with all of them the instant of submergence into the Will. And saw in the darkness a deep purple glow on the horizon – which grew in intensity until it became an all-encompassing red brilliance. And went into it, though unworthy, unclean, flesh-trapped, accepting fully the communion offered and wishing no other state of being than this divorce from self.

And was purified.

And wakened alone.

5

I KNEW Afreek well. When still a young man I had settled in the continent's dark heart for many years. Out of restlessness I had left, finally, going as far north as Agupt, where the antique relics of First Cycle days have survived better than anywhere else. In those days antiquity held no interest for me, however. I did my Watching and went about from place to place, since a Watcher does not need to have a fixed station; and chance brought me in contact with Avluela just as I was ready to roam again, and so I left Agupt for Roum and then Perris.

Now I had come back with Olmayne. We kept close to the coast and avoided the sandy inland wastes. As Pilgrims we were immune from most of the hazards of travel: we would never go hungry or without shelter, even in a place where no lodge for our guild existed, and all owed us respect. Olmayne's great beauty might have been a hazard to her, traveling as she was with no escort other than a shriveled old man, but behind the mask and robe of a Pilgrim she was safe. We unmasked only rarely, and never where we might be seen.

I had no illusions about my importance to Olmayne. To her I was merely part of the equipment of a journey – someone to help her in her communions and rituals, to arrange for lodgings, to smooth her way for her. That role suited me. She was, I knew, a dangerous woman, given to strange whims and unpredictable fancies. I wanted no entanglements with her.

She lacked a Pilgrim's purity. Even though she had passed the test of the starstone, she had not triumphed – as a Pilgrim must – over her own flesh. She slipped off, sometimes, for half a night or longer, and I pictured her lying maskless in some alley gasping in a Servitor's arms. That was her affair entirely; I never spoke of her absences upon her return.

Within our lodgings, too, she was careless of her virtue.

147

We never shared a room – no Pilgrim hostelry would permit it – but we usually had adjoining ones, and she summoned me to hers or came to mine whenever the mood took her. Often as not she was unclothed; she attained the height of the grotesque one night in Agupt when I found her wearing only her mask, all her gleaming white flesh belying the intent of the bronze grillwork that hid her face. Only once did it seem to occur to her that I might ever have been young enough to feel desire. She looked my scrawny, shrunken body over and said, 'How will you look, I wonder, when you've been renewed in Jorslem? I'm trying to picture you young, Tomis. Will you give me pleasure then?'

'I gave pleasure in my time,' I said obliquely.

Olmayne disliked the heat and dryness of Agupt. We traveled mainly by night and clung to our hostelries by day. The roads were crowded at all hours. The press of Pilgrims towards Jorslem was extraordinarily heavy, it appeared. Olmayne and I speculated on how long it might take us to gain access to the waters at such a time.

'You've never been renewed before?' she asked.

'Never.'

'Nor I. They say they don't admit all who come.'

'Renewal is a privilege, not a right,' I said. 'Many are turned away.'

'I understand also,' said Olmayne, 'that not all who enter the waters are successfully renewed.'

'I know little of this.'

'Some grow older instead of younger. Some grow young too fast, and perish. There are risks.'

'Would you not take those risks?'

She laughed. 'Only a fool would hesitate.'

'You are in no need of renewal at this time,' I pointed out. 'You were sent to Jorslem for the good of your soul, not that of your body, as I recall.'

'I'll tend to my soul as well, when I'm in Jorslem.'

'But you talk as if the house of renewal is the only shrine you mean to visit.'

'It's the important one,' she said. She rose, flexing her supple body voluptuously. 'True, I have atoning to do. But do you think I've come all the way to Jorslem just for the sake of my spirit?'

148

'I have,' I pointed out.

'*You!* You're old and withered! You'd better look after your spirit – and your flesh as well. I wouldn't mind shedding some age, though. I won't have them take off much. Eight, ten years, that's all. The years I wasted with that fool Elegro. I don't need a full renewal. You're right: I'm still in my prime.' Her face clouded. 'If the city is full of Pilgrims, maybe they won't let me into the house of renewal at all! They'll say I'm too young – tell me to come back in forty or fifty years – Tomis, would they do that to me?'

'It is hard for me to say.'

She trembled. 'They'll let *you* in. You're a walking corpse already – they have to renew you! But me – Tomis, I won't let them turn me away! If I have to pull Jorslem down stone by stone, I'll get in somehow!'

I wondered privately if her soul were in fit condition for one who poses as a candidate for renewal. Humility is recommended when one becomes a Pilgrim. But I had no wish to feel Olmayne's fury, and I kept my silence. Perhaps they would admit her to renewal despite her flaws. I had concerns of my own. It was vanity that drove Olmayne; my goals were different. I had wandered long and done much, not all of it virtuous; I needed a cleansing of my conscience in the holy city more, perhaps, than I did a lessening of my years.

Or was it only vanity for me to think so?'

6

SEVERAL days eastward of that place, as Olmayne and I walked through a parched countryside, village children chattering in fear and excitement rushed upon us.

'Please, come, come!' they cried. 'Pilgrims, come!'

Olmayne looked bewildered and irritated as they plucked at her robes. 'What are they saying, Tomis? I can't get through their damnable Aguptan accents!'

'They want us to help,' I said. I listened to their shouts. 'In their village,' I told Olmayne, 'there is an outbreak of the crystallization disease. They wish us to seek the mercies of the Will upon the sufferers.'

Olmayne drew back. I imagined the disdainful wince behind her mask. She flicked out her hands, trying to keep the children from touching her. To me she said, 'We can't go there!'

'We must.'

'We're in a hurry! Jorslem's crowded; I don't want to waste time in some dreary village.'

'They need us, Olmayne.'

'Are we Surgeons?'

'We are Pilgrims,' I said quietly. 'The benefits we gain from that carry certain obligations. If we are entitled to the hospitality of all we meet, we must also place our souls at the free disposal of the humble. Come.'

'I won't go!'

'How will that sound in Jorslem, when you give an accounting of yourself, Olmayne?'

'It's a hideous disease. What if we get it?'

'Is that what troubles you? Trust in the Will! How can you expect renewal if your soul is so deficient in grace?'

'May you rot, Tomis,' she said in a low voice. 'When did you become so pious? You're doing this deliberately, because of what I said to you by Land Bridge. In a stupid moment I taunted you, and now you're willing to expose us both to a ghastly affliction for your revenge. Don't do it, Tomis!'

I ignored her accusation. 'The children are growing agitated, Olmayne. Will you wait here for me, or will you go to the next village and wait in the hostelry there?'

'Don't leave me alone in the middle of nowhere!'

'I have to go to the sick ones,' I said.

In the end she accompanied me – I think not out of any suddenly conceived desire to be of help, but rather out of fear that her selfish refusal might somehow be held against her in Jorslem. We came shortly to the village, which was small and decayed, for Agupt lies in a terrible hot sleep and changes little with the millennia. The contrast with the busy cities farther to the south in Afreek — cities that prosper on the output of luxuries from their great Manufactories — is vast.

Shivering with heat, we followed the children to the houses of sickness.

The crystallization disease is an unlovely gift from the stars. Not many afflictions of outworlders affect the Earth-born; but from the worlds of the Spear came this ailment, carried by alien tourists, and the disease has settled among us. If it had come during the glorious days of the Second Cycle we might have eradicated it in a day; but our skills are dulled now, and no year has been without its outbreak. Olmayne was plainly terrified as we entered the first of the clay huts where the victims were kept.

There is no hope for one who has contracted this disease. One merely hopes that the healthy will be spared; and fortunately it is not a highly contagious disease. It works insidiously, transmitted in an unknown way, often failing to pass from husband to wife and leaping instead to the far side of a city, to another land entirely, perhaps. The first symptom is a scaliness of the skin; itch, flakes upon the clothing, inflammation. There follows a weakness in the bones as the calcium is dissolved. One grows limp and rubbery, but this is still an early phase. Soon the outer tissues harden. Thick, opaque membranes form on the surface of the eyes; the nostrils may close and seal; the skin grows coarse and pebbled. In this phase prophecy is common. The sufferer partakes of the skills of a Somnambulist, and utters oracles. The soul may wander, separating from the body for hours at a time, although the life-processes continue. Next, within twenty days after the onset of the disease, the crystallization ocurrs. While the skeletal structure dissolves, the skin splits and cracks, forming shining crystals in rigid geometrical patterns. The victim is quite beautiful at this time and takes on the appearance of a replica of himself in precious gems. The crystals glow with rich inner lights, violet and green and red; their sharp facets adopt new alignments from hour to hour; the slightest illumination in the room causes the sufferer to give off brilliant glittering reflections that dazzle and delight the eye. All this time the internal body is changing, as if some strange chrysalis is forming. Miraculously the organs sustain life throughout every transformation, although in the crystalline phase the victim is no longer able to communicate with others and possibly is unaware of the changes in himself. Ultimately the metamorphosis reaches the vital organs, and the process fails. The alien infestation is unable to reshape those organs without killing its host. The crisis is swift: a brief convulsion, a final discharge of energy along the nervous system of the crystallized one, and there is a quick arching of the body, accompanied by the delicate tinkling sounds of shivering glass, and then all is over. On the planet to which this is native, crystallization is not a disease but an actual metamorphosis, the result of thousands of years of evolution toward a symbiotic relationship. Unfortunately, among the Earthborn, the evolutionary preparation did not take place, and the agent of change invariably brings its subject to a fatal outcome.

Since the process is irreversible, Olmayne and I could do nothing of real value here except offer consolation to these ignorant and frightened people. I saw at once that the disease had seized this village some time ago. There were people in all stages, from the first rash to the ultimate crystallization. They were arranged in the hut according to the intensity of their infestation. To my left was a sombre row of new victims, fully conscious and morbidly scratching their arms as they contemplated the horrors that awaited them. Along the rear wall were five pallets on which lay villagers in the coarse-skinned and prophetic phase. To my right were those in varying degrees of crystallization, and up front, the diadem of the lot, was one who clearly was in his last hours of life. His body, encrusted with false emeralds and rubies and opals, shimmered in almost painful beauty; he scarcely moved; within that shell of wondrous color he was lost in some dream of ecstasy, finding at the end of his days more passion, more delight, than he could ever have known in all his harsh peasant years.

Olmayne shied back from the door.

'It's horrible,' she whispered. 'I won't go in!'

'We must. We are under an obligation.'

'I never wanted to be a Pilgrim!'

'You wanted atonement,' I reminded her. 'It must be earned.'

'We'll catch the disease!'

'The Will can reach us anywhere to infect us with this, Olmayne. It strikes at random. The danger is no greater for us inside this building than it is in Perris.'

'Why, then, are so many in this one village smitten?'

'This village has earned the displeasure of the Will.'

'How neatly you serve up the mysticism, Tomis,' she said bitterly. 'I misjudged you. I thought you were a sensible man. This fatalism of yours is ugly.'

'I watched my world conquered,' I said. 'I beheld the Prince of Roum destroyed. Calamities breed such attitudes as I now have. Let us go in, Olmayne.'

We entered, Olmayne still reluctant. Now fear assailed me, but I concealed it. I had been almost smug in my piety while arguing with the lovely Rememberer woman who was my companion, but I could not deny the sudden seething of fright.

I forced myself to be tranquil.

There are redemptions and redemptions, I told myself. If this disease is to be the source of mine, I will abide by the Will.

Perhaps Olmayne came to some such decision too, as we went in, or maybe her own sense of the dramatic forced her into the unwanted role of the lady of mercy. She made the rounds with me. We passed from pallet to pallet, heads bowed, starstones in our hands. We said words. We smiled when the newly sick begged for reassurance. We offered prayers. Olmayne paused before one girl in the secondary phase, whose eyes already were filming over with horny tissue, and knelt and touched her starstone to the girl's scaly cheek. The girl spoke in oracles, but unhappily not in any language we understood.

153

At last we came to the terminal case, he who had grown his own superb sarcophagus. Somehow I felt purged of fear, and so too was Ōlmayne, for we stood a long while before this grotesque sight, silent, and then she whispered, 'How terrible! How wonderful! How beautiful!'

Three more huts similar to this one awaited us.

The villagers clustered at the doorways. As we emerged from each building in turn, the healthy ones fell down about us, clutching at the hems of our robes, stridently demanding that we intercede for them with the Will. We spoke such words as seemed appropriate and not too insincere. Those within the huts received our words blankly, as if they already realized there was no chance for them; those outside, still untouched by the disease, clung to every syllable. The headman of the village – only an acting headman; the true chief lay crystallized – thanked us again and again, as though we had done something real. At least we had given comfort, which is not to be despised.

When we came forth from the last of the sickhouses, we saw a slight figure watching us from a distance: the Changeling Bernalt. Olmayne nudged me.

'That creature has been following us, Tomis. All the way from Land Bridge!'

'He travels to Jorslem also.'

'Yes, but why should he stop here? Why in this awful place?'

'Hush, Olmayne. Be civil to him now.'

'To a *Changeling?*'

Bernalt approached. The mutated one was clad in a soft white robe that blunted the strangeness of his appearance. He nodded sadly toward the village and said, 'A great tragedy. The Will lies heavily on this place.'

He explained that he had arrived here several days ago and had met a friend from his native city of Nayrub. I assumed he meant a Changeling, but no, Bernalt's friend was a Surgeon, he said, who had halted here to do what he could for the afflicted villagers. The idea of a friendship between a Changeling and a Surgeon seemed a bit odd to me, and positively contemptible to Olmayne, who did not trouble to hide her loathing of Bernalt.

A partly crystallized figure staggered from one of the huts, gnarled hands clutching. Bernalt went forward and

154

gently guided it back within. Returning to us, he said, 'There are times one is actually glad one is a Changeling. That disease does not affect us, you know.' His eyes acquired a sudden glitter. 'Am I forcing myself on you, Pilgrims? You seem like stone behind your masks. I mean no harm; shall I withdraw?'

'Of course not,' I said, meaning the opposite. His company disturbed me; perhaps the ordinary disdain for Changelings was a contagion that had at last reached me. 'Stay awhile. I would ask you to travel with us to Jorslem, but you know it is forbidden for us.'

'Certainly. I quite understand.' He was coolly polite, but the seething bitterness in him was close to the surface. Most Changelings are such degraded bestial things that they are incapable of knowing how detested they are by normal guilded men and women; but Bernalt clearly was gifted with the torment of comprehension. He smiled, and then he pointed. 'My friend is here.'

Three figures approached. One was Bernalt's Surgeon, a slender man, dark-skinned, soft-voiced, with weary eyes and sparse yellow hair. With him were an official of the invaders and another outworlder from a different planet. 'I had heard that two Pilgrims were summoned to this place,' said the invader. 'I am grateful for the comfort you may have brought these sufferers. I am Earthclaim Nineteen; this district is under my administration. Will you be my guests at dinner this night?'

I was doubtful of taking an invader's hospitality, and Olmayne's sudden clenching of her fist over her starstone told me that she also hesitated. Earthclaim Nineteen seemed eager for our acceptance. He was not as tall as most of his kind, and his malproportioned arms reached below his knees. Under the blazing Aguptan sun his thick waxy skin acquired a high gloss, although he did not perspire.

Into a long, tense, and awkward silence the Surgeon inserted: 'No need to hold back. In this village we all are brothers. Join us tonight, will you?'

We did. Earthclaim Nineteen occupied a villa by the shore of Lake Medit; in the clear light of late afternoon I thought I could detect Land Bridge jutting forward to my left, and even Eyrop at the far side of the lake. We were waited upon by members of the guild of Servitors who brought us cool drinks on the patio. The invader had a large staff, all Earthborn; to me it was another sign that our conquest had become institutionalized and was wholly accepted by the bulk of the populace. Until long after dusk we talked, lingering over drinks even as the writhing auroras danced into view to herald the night. Bernalt the Changeling remained apart, though, perhaps ill at ease in our presence. Olmayne too was moody and withdrawn; a mingled depression and exaltation had settled over her in the stricken village, and the presence of Bernalt at the dinner party had reinforced her silence, for she had no idea how to be polite in the presence of a Changeling. The invader, our host, was charming and attentive, and tried to bring her forth from her bleakness. I had seen charming conquerors before. I had traveled with one who had posed as the Earthborn Changeling Gormon in the days just before the conquest. This one, Earthclaim Nineteen, had been a poet on his native world in those days. I said, 'It seems unlikely that one of your inclinations would care to be part of a military occupation.'

'All experiences strengthen the art,' said Earthclaim Nineteen. 'I seek to expand myself. In any case I am not a warrior but an administrator. Is it so strange that a poet can be an administrator, or an administrator a poet?' He laughed. 'Among your many guilds, there is no guild of Poets. Why?'

'There are Communicants,' I said. 'They serve your muse.'

'But in a religious way. They are interpreters of the Will, not of their own souls.'

'The two are indistinguishable. The verses they make are divinely inspired, but rise from the hearts of their makers,' I said.

Earthclaim Nineteen looked unconvinced. 'You may argue that all poetry is at bottom religious, I suppose. But this stuff of your Communicants is too limited in scope. It deals only with acquiescence to the Will.'

'A paradox,' said Olmayne. 'The Will encompasses everything, and yet you say that our Communicants' scope is limited.'

'There are other themes for poetry besides immersion in the Will, my friends. The love of person for person, the joy of defending one's home, the wonder of standing naked beneath the fiery stars—' The invader laughed. 'Can it be that Earth fell so swiftly because its only poets were poets of acquiescence to destiny?'

'Earth fell,' said the Surgeon, 'because the Will required us to atone for the sin our ancestors committed when they treated your ancestors like beasts. The quality of our poetry had nothing to do with it.'

'The Will decreed that you would lose to us by way of punishment, eh? But if the Will is omnipotent, it must have decreed the sin of your ancestors that made the punishment necessary. Eh? Eh? The Will playing games with itself. You see the difficulty of believing in a divine force that determines all events? Where is the element of choice that makes suffering meaningful? To force you into a sin, and then to require you to endure as atonement, seems to me an empty exercise. Forgive my blasphemy.'

The Surgeon said, 'You misunderstand. All that has happened on this planet is part of a process of moral instruction. The Will does not shape every event great or small; it provides the raw material of events, and allows us to follow such patterns as we desire.'

'Example?'

'The Will imbued the Earthborn with skills and knowledge. During the First Cycle we rose from savagery in little time; in the Second Cycle we attained greatness. In our moment of greatness we grew swollen with pride, choosing to exceed our limitations. We imprisoned intelligent creatures of other worlds under the pretense of "study," when we acted really out of an arrogant desire for amusement, and we toyed with our world's climate until oceans joined and continents sank and our old civilization was destroyed. Thus the Will instructed us in the boundaries of human ambition.'

'I dislike that dark philosophy even more,' said Earthclaim Nineteen. 'I—'

'Let me finish,' said the Surgeon. 'The collapse of Second Cycle Earth was our punishment. The defeat of Third Cycle Earth by you folk from the stars is a completion of that earlier punishment, but also the beginning of a new phase. You are the instruments of our redemption. By inflicting on us the final humiliation of conquest, you bring us to

157

the bottom of our trough; now we renew our souls, now we begin to rise, tested by adversities.'

I stared in sudden amazement at this Surgeon, who was uttering ideas that been stirring in me all along the road to Jorslem, ideas of redemption both personal and planetary. I had paid little attention to the Surgeon before.

'Permit me a statement,' Bernalt said suddenly, his first words in hours.

We looked at him. The pigmented bands in his face were ablaze, marking his emotion.

He said, nodding to the Surgeon, 'My friend, you speak of redemption for the Earthborn. Do you mean *all* Earthborn, or only the guilded ones?'

'All Earthborn, of course,' said the Surgeon mildly. 'Are we not all equally conquered?'

'We are not equal in other things, though. Can there be redemption for a planet that keeps millions of its people thrust into guildlessness? I speak of my own folk, of course. We sinned long ago when we thought we were striking out against those who had created us as monsters. We strove to take Jorslem from you; and for this we were punished, and our punishment has lasted for a thousand years. We are still outcasts, are we not? Where has our hope of redemption been? Can you guilded ones consider yourself purified and made virtuous by your recent suffering, when you still step on us?'

The Surgeon looked dismayed. 'You speak rashly, Bernalt. I know that Changelings have a grievance. But you know as well as I that the time of deliverance is at hand. In the days to come no Earthborn one will scorn you, and you will stand beside us when we regain our freedom.'

Bernalt peered at the floor. 'Forgive me, my friend. Of course, of course, you speak the truth. I was carried away. The heat – this splendid wine – how foolishly I spoke!'

Earthclaim Nineteen said, 'Are you telling me that a resistance movement is forming that will shortly drive us from your planet?'

'I speak only in abstract terms,' said the Surgeon.

'I think your resistance movement will be purely abstract too,' the invader replied easily. 'Forgive me, but I see little strength in a planet that could be conquered in a single night. We expect our occupation of Earth to be a long one and to meet little opposition. In the months that we have been here there has been no sign of increasing hostility to us. Quite the contrary: we are increasingly accepted among you.'

'It is part of a process,' said the Surgeon. 'As a poet, you should understand that words carry meanings of many kinds. We do not need to overthrow our alien masters in order to be free of them. Is that poetic enough for you?'

'Splendid,' said Earthclaim Nineteen, getting to his feet. 'Shall we go to dinner now?'

7

THERE was no way to return to the subject. A philosophical discussion at the dinner table is difficult to sustain; and our host did not seem comfortable with this analysis of Earth's destinies. Swiftly he discovered that Olmayne had been a Rememberer before turning Pilgrim, and thereafter directed his words to her, questioning her on our history and our early poetry. Like most invaders he had a fierce curiosity concerning our past. Olmayne gradually came out of the silence that gripped her, and spoke at length about her researches in Perris. She talked with great familiarity of our hidden past, with Earthclaim Nineteen occasionally inserting an intelligent and informed question; meanwhile we dined on delicacies of a number of worlds, perhaps imported by the same fat, insensitive Merchant who had driven us from Perris to Marsay; the villa was cool and the Servitors attentive; that miserable plague-stricken peasant village half an hour's walk away might well have been in some other galaxy, so remote was it from our discourse now.

When we left the villa in the morning, the Surgeon asked permission to join our Pilgrimage. 'There is nothing further I can do here,' he explained. 'At the outbreak of the disease I came up from my home in Nayrub, and I've been here many days, more to console than to cure, of course. Now I am called to Jorslem. However, if it violates your vows to have company on the road—'

'By all means come with us,' I said.

'There will be one other companion,' the Surgeon told us.

He meant the third person who had met us at the village: the outworlder, an enigma, yet to say a word in our presence. This being was a flattened spike-shaped creature somewhat taller than a man and mounted on a jointed tripod of angular legs; it place of origin was in the Golden Spiral; its skin was rough and bright red in hue, and vertical rows of glassy oval eyes descended on three sides from the top of its tapered head. I had never seen such a creature before. It had come to Earth, according to the Surgeon, on a data-gathering mission, and had already roamed much of Ais and Stralya. Now it was touring the lands on the margin of Lake Medit; and after seeing Jorslem it would depart for the great cities of Eyrop. Solemn, unsettling in its perpetual watchfulness, never blinking its many eyes nor offering a comment on what those eyes beheld, it seemed more like some odd machine, some information-intake for a memory tank, than a living creature. But it was harmless enough to let it come with us to the holy city.

The Surgeon bade farewell to his Changeling friend, who went on alone ahead of us, and paid a final call on the crystallized village. We stayed back, since there was no point in our going. When he returned, his face was somber. 'Four new cases,' he said. 'This entire village will perish. There has never been an outbreak of this kind before on Earth – so concentrated an epidemic.'

'Something new, then?' I asked. 'Will it spread everywhere?'

'Who knows? No one in the adjoining village has caught it. The pattern is unfamiliar: a single village wholly devastated, and nowhere else besides. These people see it as divine retribution for unknown sins.'

'What could peasants have done,' I asked, 'that would bring the wrath of the Will so harshly upon them?'

'They are asking that too,' said the Surgeon.

Olmayne said, 'If there are new cases, our visit yesterday was useless. We risked ourselves and did them no good.'

'Wrong,' the Surgeon told her. 'These cases were already incubating when we arrived. We may hope that the disease will not spread to those who still were in full health.'

He did not seem confident of that.

Olmayne examined herself from day to day for symptoms of the disease, but none appeared. She gave the Surgeon much trouble on that score, bothering him for opinions concerning real or fancied blemishes of her skin, embarrassing him by removing her mask in his presence so that he could determine that some speck on her cheek was not the first trace of crystallization.

The Surgeon took all this in good grace, for, while the outworld being was merely a cipher plodding alongside us,

161

the Surgeon was a man of depth, patience and sophistication. He was native to Afreek, and had been dedicated to his guild at birth by his father, since healing was the family tradition. Traveling widely, he had seen most of our world and had forgotten little of what he had seen. He spoke to us of Roum and Perris, of the frostflower fields of Stralya, of my own birthplace in the western island group of the Lost Continents. He questioned us tactfully about our starstones and the effects they produced – I could see he hungered to try the stone himself, but that of course was forbidden to one who had not declared himself a Pilgrim – and when he learned that in former life I had been a Watcher, he asked me a great deal concerning the instruments by which I had scanned the heavens, wishing to know what it was I perceived and how I imagined the perception was accomplished. I spoke to him as fully as I could on these matters, though in truth I knew little.

Usually we kept on the green strip of fertile land bordering the lake, but once, at the Surgeon's insistence, we detoured into the choking desert to see something that he promised would be of interest. He would not tell us what it was. We were at this point traveling in hired rollerwagons, open on top, and sharp winds blew gusts of sand in our faces. Sand adhered briefly to the outworlder's eyes, I saw; and I saw how efficiently it flushed each eye with a flood of blue tears every few moments. The rest of us huddled in our garments, heads down, whenever the wind arose.

'We are here,' the Surgeon announced finally. 'When I traveled with my father I first visited this place long ago. We will go inside – and then you, the former Rememberer, will tell us where we are.'

It was a building two stories high made of bricks of white glass. The doors appeared sealed, but they gave at the slightest pressure. Lights glowed into life the moment we entered.

In long aisles, lightly strewn with sand, were tables on which instruments were mounted. Nothing was comprehensible to me. There were devices shaped like hands, into which one's own hand could be inserted; conduits led from the strange metal gloves to shining closed cabinets, and arrangements of mirrors transmitted images from the interiors of those cabinets to giant screens overhead. The Surgeon placed his hands in the gloves and moved his fingers; the screens brightened, and I saw images of tiny needles moving through shallow arcs. He went to other machines and released dribbles of unknown fluids; he touched small buttons and produced musical sounds; he moved freely through a laboratory of wonders, clearly ancient, which seemed still in order and awaiting the return of its users.

Olmayne was ecstatic. She followed the Surgeon from aisle to aisle, handling everything.

'Well, Rememberer?' he asked finally. 'What is this?'

'A Surgery,' she said in lowered voice. 'A Surgery of the Years of Magic!'

'Exactly! Splendid!' He seemed in an oddly excited state. 'We could make dazzling monsters here! We could work miracles! Fliers, Swimmers, Changelings, Twiners, Burners, Climbers – invent your own guilds, shape men to your whims! This was the place!'

Olmayne said, 'These Surgeries have been described to me. There are six of them left, are there not, one in northern Eyrop, one on Palash, one here, one far to the south in Deeper Afreek, one in western Ais—' She faltered.

'And one in Hind, the greatest of all!' said the Surgeon.

'Yes, of course, Hind! The home of the Fliers!'

Their awe was contagious. I said, 'This was where the shapes of men were changed? How was it done?'

The Surgeon shrugged. 'The art is lost. The Years of Magic were long ago, old man.'

'Yes, yes, I know. But surely if the equipment survives, we could guess how—'

'With these knives,' said the Surgeon, 'we cut into the fabric of the unborn, editing the human seed. The Surgeon placed his hands here – he manipulated – and within that incubator the knives did their work. Out of this came Fliers and all the rest. The forms bred true. Some are extinct today, but our Fliers and our Changelings owe their heritage to some such building as this. The Changelings, of course, were the Surgeons' mistakes. They should not have been permitted to live.'

'I thought that these monsters were the products of teratogenic drugs given to them when they still were within the womb,' I said. 'You tell me now that Changelings were made by Surgeons. Which is so?'

163

'Both,' he replied. 'All Changelings today are descended from the flaws and errors committed by the Surgeons of the Years of Magic. Yet mothers in that unhappy group often enhance the monstrousness of their children with drugs, so that they will be more marketable. It is an ugly tribe not merely in looks. Small wonder that their guild was dissolved and they were thrust outside society. We—'

Something bright flew through the air, missing his face by less than a hand's breadth. He dropped to the floor and shouted to us to take cover. As I fell I saw a second missile fly toward us. The outworld being, still observing all phenomena, studied it impassively in the moment of life that remained to it. Then the weapon struck two thirds of the way up the outworlder's body and severed it instantly. Other missiles followed, clattering against the wall behind us. I saw our attackers: a band of Changelings, fierce, hideous. We were unarmed. They moved toward us. I readied myself to die.

From the doorway a voice cried out: a familiar voice, using the thick and unfamiliar words of the language Changelings speak among themselves. Instantly the assault ceased. Those who menaced us turned toward the door. The Changeling Bernalt entered.

'I saw your vehicle,' he said. 'I thought you might be here, and perhaps in trouble. It seems I came in time.'

'Not altogether,' said the Surgeon. He indicated the fallen outworlder, which was beyond all aid. 'But why this attack?'

Bernalt gestured. '*They* will tell you.'

We looked at the five Changelings who had ambushed us. They were not of the educated, civilized sort such as Bernalt, nor were any two of them of the same styles; each was a twisted, hunched mockery of the human form, one with ropy tendrils descending from his chin, one with a face that was a featureless void, another whose ears were giant cups, and so forth. From the one closest to us, a creature with small platforms jutting from his skin in a thousand places, we learned why we had been assaulted. In a brutal Aguptan dialect he told us that we had profaned a temple sacred to Changelings. 'We keep out of Jorslem,' he told us. 'Why must you come here?'

Of course he was right. We asked forgiveness as sincerely as we could, and the Surgeon explained that he had visited

164

this place long ago and it had not been a temple then. That seemed to soothe the Changeling, who admitted that only in recent years had his kind used it as a shrine. He was soothed even more when Olmayne opened the overpocket fastened between her breasts and offered a few glittering gold coins, part of the treasure she had brought with her from Perris. The bizarre and deformed beings were satisfied at that and allowed us to leave the building. We would have taken the dead outworlder with us, but during our parley with the Changelings the body had nearly vanished, nothing but a faint gray streak remaining on the sandy floor to tell us where it had fallen. 'A mortuary enzyme,' the Surgeon explained. 'Triggered by interruption of the life processes.'

Others of this community of desert-dwelling Changelings were lurking about outside the building as we came forth. They were a tribe of nightmares, with skin of every texture and color, facial features arranged at random, all kinds of genetic improvisations of organs and bodily accessories. Bernalt himself, although their brother, seemed appalled by their monstrousness. They looked at him with awe. At the sight of us some of them fondled the throwing weapons at their hips, but a sharp command from Bernalt prevented any trouble.

He said, 'I regret the treatment you received and the death of the outworlder. But of course it is risky to enter a place that is sacred to backward and violent people.'

'We had no idea,' the Surgeon said. 'We never would have gone in if we had realized—'

'Of course. Of course.' Was there something patronizing about Bernalt's soft, civilized tones? 'Well, again I bid you farewell.'

I blurted suddenly, 'No. Travel with us to Jorslem! It's ridiculous for us to go separately to the same place.'

Olmayne gasped. Even the Surgeon seemed amazed. Only Bernalt remained calm. He said, 'You forget, friend, that it is improper for Pilgrims to journey with the guildless. Besides, I am here to worship at this shrine, and it will take me a while. I would not wish to delay you.' His hand reached out to mine. Then he moved away, entering the ancient Surgery. Scores of his fellow Changelings rushed in after him. I was grateful to Bernalt for his tact; my impulsive offer of companionship, though sincerely meant, had been impossible for him to accept.

We boarded our rollerwagons. In a moment we heard a dreadful sound: a discordant Changeling hymn in praise of I dare not think what deity, a scraping, grinding, screeching song as misshapen as those who uttered it.

'The beasts,' Olmayne muttered. 'A sacred shrine! A Changeling temple! How loathsome! They might have killed us all, Tomis. How can such monsters have a religion?'

I made no reply. The Surgeon looked at Olmayne sadly and shook his head as though distressed by so little charity on the part of one who claimed to be a Pilgrim.

'They also are human,' he said.

At the next town along our route we reported the starborn being's death to the occupying authorities. Then, saddened and silent, we three survivors continued onward to the place where the coastline trends north rather than east. We were leaving sleepy Agupt behind and entering now into the borders of the land in which holy Jorslem lies.

8

THE city of Jorslem sits some good distance inland from Lake Medit on a cool plateau guarded by a ring of low, barren, rock-strewn mountains. All my life, it seemed, had been but a preparation for my first glimpse of this golden city, whose image I knew so well. Hence when I saw its spires and parapets rising in the east, I felt not so much awe as a sense of homecoming.

A winding road took us down through the encircling hills to the city, whose wall was made of squared blocks of a fine stone, dark pink-gold in color. The houses and shrines, too, were of this stone. Groves of trees bordered the road, nor were they star-trees, but native products of Earth, as was fitting to this, the oldest of man's cities, older than Roum, older than Perris, its roots deep in the First Cycle.

The invaders, shrewdly, had not meddled with Jorslem's administration. The city remained under the governorship of the Guildmaster of Pilgrims, and even an invader was required to seek the Guildmaster's permission to enter. Of course, this was strictly a matter of form; the Pilgrim Guildmaster, like the Chancellor of the Rememberers and other such officials, was in truth a puppet subject to our conqueror's wishes. But that harsh fact was kept concealed. The invaders had left our holy city as a city apart, and we would not see them swaggering in armed teams through Jorslem's streets.

At the outer wall we formally requested entry from the Sentinel guarding the gate. Though elsewhere most Sentinels were now unemployed – since cities stood open by command of our masters – this man was in full guild array and calmly insisted on thorough procedure. Olmayne and I, as Pilgrims, were entitled to automatic access to Jorslem; yet he made us produce our starstones as evidence that we came by our robes and masks honestly, and then donned a thinking cap to check our names with the archives of our guild. In time we met approval. The Surgeon our companion had an easier time; he had applied in advance for entry while in Afreek, and after a moment to check his identity he was admitted.

Within the walls everything had the aspect of great antiquity. Jorslem alone of the world's cities still preserves much of its First Cycle architecture: not merely broken columns and ruined aqueducts, as in Roum, but whole streets, covered arcades, towers, boulevards, that have lasted through every upheaval our world has seen. And so once we passed into the city we wandered in wonder through its strangeness, down streets paved with cobbled stones, into narrow alleys cluttered with children and beggars, across markets fragrant with spices. After an hour of this we felt it was time to seek lodgings, and here it was necessary for us to part company with the Surgeon, since he was ineligible to stay at a Pilgrim hostelry, and it would have been costly and foolish for us to stay anywhere else. We saw him to the inn where he had previously booked a room. I thanked him for his good companionship on our journey, and he thanked us just as gravely and expressed the hope that he would see us again in Jorslem in the days to come. Then Olmayne and I took leave of him and rented quarters in one of the numerous places catering to the Pilgrim trade.

The city exists solely to serve Pilgrims and casual tourists, and so it is really one vast hostelry; robed Pilgrims are as common in Jorslem's streets as Fliers in Hind. We settled and rested awhile; then we dined and afterward walked along a broad street from which we could see, to the east, Jorslem's inner and most sacred district. There is a city within a city here. The most ancient part, so small it can be traversed in less than an hour on foot, is wrapped in a high wall of its own. Therein lie shrines revered by Earth's former religions: the Christers, the Hebers, the Mislams. The place where the god of the Christers died is said to be there, but this may be a distortion wrought by time, since what kind of god is it that dies? On a high place in one corner of the Old City stands a gilded dome sacred to the Mislams, which is carefully tended by the common folk of Jorslem. And to the fore part of that high place are the huge gray blocks of a stone wall worshipped by the Hebers. These things remain, but the ideas behind

168

them are lost; never while I was among the Rememberers did I meet any scholar who could explain the merit of worshiping a wall or a gilded dome. Yet the old records assure us that these three First Cycle creeds were of great depth and richness.

In the Old City, also, is a Second Cycle place that was of much more immediate interest to Olmayne and myself. As we stared through the darkness at the holy precincts Olmayne said, 'We should make application tomorrow at the house of renewal.'

'I agree. I long now to give up some of my years.'

'Will they accept me, Tomis?'

'Speculating on it is idle,' I told her. 'We will go, and we will apply, and your question will be answered.'

She said something further, but I did not hear her words, for at that moment three Fliers passed above me, heading east. One was male, two female; they flew naked, according to the custom of their guild; and the Flier in the center of the group was a slim, fragile girl, mere bones and wings, moving with a grace that was exceptional even for her airy kind.

'*Avluela!*' I gasped.

The trio of Fliers disappeared beyond the parapets of the Old City. Stunned, shaken, I clung to a tree for support and struggled for breath.

'Tomis?' Olmayne said. 'Tomis, are you ill?'

'I know it was Avluela. They said she had gone back to Hind, but no, that was Avluela! How could I mistake her?'

'You've said that about every Flier you've seen since leaving Perris,' said Olmayne coldly.

'But this time I'm certain! Where is a thinking cap? I must check with the Fliers' Lodge at once!'

Olmayne's hand rested on my arm. 'It's late, Tomis. You act feverish. Why this excitement over your skinny Flier, anyway? What did she mean to you?'

'She—'

I halted, unable to put my meaning in words. Olmayne knew the story of my journey up out of Agupt with the girl, how as a celibate old Watcher I had conceived a kind of parental fondness for her, how I had perhaps felt something more powerful than that, how I had lost her to the false Changeling Gormon, and how *he* in turn had lost her to the Prince of Roum. But yet what was Avluela to me? Why did a glimpse of someone who merely might have been Avluela send me into this paroxysm of confusion? I chased symbols in my turbulent mind and found no answers.

'Come back to the inn and rest,' Olmayne said. 'Tomorrow we must seek renewal.'

First, though, I donned a cap and made contact with the Fliers' Lodge. My thoughts slipped through the shielding interface to the storage brain of the guild registry; I asked and received the answer I had sought. Avluela of the Fliers was indeed now a resident in Jorslem. 'Take this message for her,' I said. 'The Watcher she knew in Roum now is here as a Pilgrim, and wishes to meet her outside the house of renewal at midday tomorrow.'

With that done, I accompanied Olmayne to our lodgings. She seemed sullen and aloof; and when she unmasked in my room her face appeared rigid with – jealousy? Yes. To Olmayne all men were vassals, even one so shriveled and worn as I; and she loathed it that another woman could kindle such a flame in me. When I drew forth my starstone, Olmayne at first would not join me in communion. Only when I began the rituals did she submit. But I was so tense that night I was unable to make the merging with the Will, nor could she achieve it; and thus we faced one another glumly for half an hour, and abandoned the attempt, and parted for the night.

9

ONE must go by one's self to the house of renewal. At
dawn I awoke, made a brief and more successful communion,
and set out unbreakfasted, without Olmayne. In half an
hour I stood before the golden wall of the Old City; in
half an hour more I had finished my crossing of the inner
city's tangled lanes. Passing before that gray wall so dear
to the ancient Hebers, I went up onto the high place; I
passed near the gilded dome of the vanished Mislams and,
turning to the left, followed the stream of Pilgrims which
already at this early hour was proceeding to the house of
renewal.

This house is a Second Cycle building, for it was then
that the renewal process was conceived; and of all that
era's science, only renewal has come down to us approxi-
mately as it must have been practiced in that time. Like
those other few Second Cycle structures that survive, the
house of renewal is supple and sleek, architecturally under-
stated, with deft curves and smooth textures; it is without
windows; it bears no external ornament whatever. There
are many doors. I placed myself before the easternmost
entrance, and in an hour's time I was admitted.

Just inside the entrance I was greeted by a green-robed
member of the guild of Renewers – the first member of
this guild I had ever seen. Renewers are recruited entirely
from Pilgrims who are willing to make it their life's work
to remain in Jorslem and aid others toward renewal. Their
guild is under the same administration as the Pilgrims; a
single guildmaster directs the destinies of both; even the
garb is the same except for color. In effect Pilgrims and
Renewers are of one guild and represent different phases
of the same affiliation. But a distinction is always drawn.

The Renewer's voice was light and cheerful. 'Welcome to
this house, Pilgrim. Who are you, where are you from?'

'I am the Pilgrim Tomis, formerly Tomis of the Rememberers, and prior to that a Watcher, born to the name

171

Wuellig. I am native to the Lost Continents and have traveled widely both before and after beginning my Pilgrimage.'

'What do you seek here?'

'Renewal. Redemption.'

'May the Will grant your wishes,' said the Renewer. 'Come with me.'

I was led through a close, dimly lit passage into a small stone cell. The Renewer instructed me to remove my mask, enter into a state of communion, and wait. I freed myself from the bronze grillwork and clasped my starstone tightly. The familiar sensations of communion stole over me, but no union with the Will took place; rather, I felt a specific link forming with the mind of another human being. Although mystified, I offered no resistance.

Something probed my soul. Everything was drawn forth and laid out as if for inspection on the floor of the cell: my acts of selfishness and of cowardice, my flaws and failings, my doubts, my despairs, above all the most shameful of my acts, the selling of the Rememberers' document to the invader overlord. I beheld these things and knew that I was unworthy of renewal. In this house one might extend one's lifetime two or three times over; but why should the Renewers offer such benefits to anyone as lacking in merit as I?

I remained a long while in contemplation of my faults. Then the contact broke, and a different Rememberer, a man of remarkable stature, entered the cell.

'The mercy of the Will is upon you, friend,' he said, reaching forth fingers of extraordinary length to touch the tips of mine.

When I heard that deep voice and saw those white fingers, I knew that I was in the presence of a man I had met briefly before, as I stood outside the gates of Roum in the season before the conquest of Earth. He had been a Pilgrim then, and he had invited me to join him on his journey to Jorslem, but I had declined, for Roum had beckoned to me.

'Was your Pilgrimage an easy one?' I asked.

'It was a valuable one,' he replied. 'And you? You are a Watcher no longer, I see.'

'I am in my third guild this year.'

'With one more yet to come,' he said.

'Am I to join you in the Renewers, then?'

'I did not mean that guild, friend Tomis. But we can talk more of that when your years are fewer. You have been approved for renewal, I rejoice to tell you.'

'Despite my sins?'

'Because of your sins, such that they are. At dawn tomorrow you enter the first of the renewal tanks. I will be your guide through your second birth. I am the Renewer Talmit. Go, now, and ask for me when you return.'

'One question—'

'Yes?'

'I made my Pilgrimage together with a woman, Olmayne, formerly a Rememberer of Perris. Can you tell me if she has been approved for renewal as well?'

'I know nothing of this Olmayne.'

'She's not a good woman,' I said. 'She is vain, imperious, and cruel. But yet I think she is not beyond saving. Can you do anything to help her?'

'I have no influence in such things,' Talmit said. 'She must face interrogation like everyone else. I can tell you this, though: virtue is not the only criterion for renewal.'

He showed me from the building. Cold sunlight illuminated the city. I was drained and depleted, too empty even to feel cheered that I had qualified for renewal. It was midday; I remembered my appointment with Avluela; I circled the house of renewal in rising anxiety. Would she come?

She was waiting by the front of the building, beside a glittering monument from Second Cycle days. Crimson jacket, furry leggings, glass bubbles on her feet, telltale humps on her back: from afar I could make her out to be a Flier. 'Avluela!' I called.

She whirled. She looked pale, thin, even younger than when I had last seen her. Her eyes searched my face, once again masked, and for a moment she was bewildered.

'Watcher?' she said. 'Watcher, is that you?'

'Call me Tomis now,' I told her. 'But I am the same man you knew in Agupt and Roum.'

'Watcher! Oh, Watcher! *Tomis.*' She clung to me. 'How long it's been! So much has happened!' She sparkled now, and the paleness fled her cheeks. 'Come, let's find an inn, a place to sit and talk! How did you discover me here?'

173

'Through your guild. I saw you overhead last night.'

'I came here in the winter. I was in Pars for a while, halfway back to Hind, and then I changed my mind. There could be no going home. Now I live near Jorslem and I help with—' She cut her sentence sharply off. 'Have you won renewal, Tomis?'

We descended from the high place into a humbler part of the inner city. 'Yes,' I said, 'I am to be made younger. My guide is the Renewer Talmit – we met him as a Pilgrim outside Roum, do you remember?'

She had forgotten that. We seated ourselves at an open-air patio adjoining an inn, and Servitors brought us food and wine. Her gaiety was infectious; I felt renewed just to be with her. She spoke of those final cataclysmic days in Roum, when she had been taken into the palace of the Prince as a concubine; and she told me of that terrible moment when Gormon the Changeling defeated the Prince of Roum on the evening of the conquest – announcing himself as no Changeling but an invader in disguise, and taking from the Prince at once his throne, his concubine, and his vision.

'Did the Prince die?' she asked.

'Yes, but not of his blinding.' I told her how that proud man had fled Roum disguised as a Pilgrim, and how I had accompanied him to Perris, and how, while we were among the Rememberers, he had involved himself with Olmayne, and had been slain by Olmayne's husband, whose life was thereupon taken by his wife. 'I also saw Gormon in Perris,' I said. 'He goes by the name of Victorious Thirteen now. He is high in the councils of the invaders.'

Avluela smiled. 'Gormon and I were together only a short while after the conquest. He wanted to tour Eyrop; I flew with him to Donsk and Sved, and there he lost interest in me. It was then that I felt I must go home to Hind, but later I changed my mind. When does your renewal begin?'

'At dawn.'

'Oh, Tomis, how will it be when you are a young man? Did you know that I loved you? All the time we traveled, all while I was sharing Gormon's bed and consorting with the Prince, you were the one I wanted! But of course you were a Watcher, and it was impossible. Besides, you were so old. Now you no longer Watch, and soon you will no longer be old, and—' Her hand rested on mine. 'I should never have left your side. We both would have been spared much suffering.'

'We learn, from suffering,' I said.

'Yes. Yes. I see that. How long will your renewal take?'

'The usual time, whatever that may be.'

'After that, what will you do? What guild will you choose? You can't be a Watcher, not now.'

'No, nor a Rememberer either. My guide Talmit spoke of some other guild, which he would not name, and assumed that I would enroll in it when I was done with renewal. I supposed he thought I'd stay here and join the Renewers, but he said it was another guild.'

'Not the Renewers,' said Avluela. She leaned close. 'The Redeemers,' she whispered.

'Redeemers? That is a guild I do not know.'

'It is newly founded.'

'No new guild has been established in more than a—'

'This is the guild Talmit meant. You would be a desirable member. The skills you developed when you were a Watcher make you exceptionally useful.'

'Redeemers,' I said, probing the mystery. '*Redeemers*. What does this guild do?'

Avluela smiled jauntily. 'It rescues troubled souls and saves unhappy worlds. But this is no time to talk of it. Finish your business in Jorslem, and everything will become clear.' We rose. Her lips brushed mine. 'This is the last time I'll see you as an old man. It will be strange, Tomis, when you're renewed!'

She left me then.

Toward evening I returned to my lodging. Olmayne was not in her room. A Servitor told me that she had been out all day. I waited until it was late; then I made my communion and slept, and at dawn I paused outside her door. It was sealed. I hurried to the house of renewal.

10

THE RENEWER Talmit met me within the entrance and conducted me down a corridor of green tile to the first renewal tank. 'The Pilgrim Olmayne,' he informed me, 'has been accepted for renewal and will come here later this day.' This was the last reference to the affairs of another human being that I was to hear for some time. Talmit showed me into a small low room, close and humid, lit by dim blobs of slavelight and smelling faintly of crushed deathflower blossoms. My robe and my mask were taken from me, and the Renewer covered my head with a fine golden-green mesh of some flimsy metal, through which he sent a current; and when he removed the mesh, my hair was gone, my head was as glossy as the tiled walls. 'It makes insertion of the electrodes simpler,' Talmit explained. 'You may enter the tank, now.'

A gentle ramp led me down into the tank, which was a tub of no great size. I felt the warm soft slipperiness of mud beneath my feet, and Talmit nodded and told me it irradiated regenerative mud, which would stimulate the increase of cell division that was to bring about my renewal, and I accepted it. I stretched out on the floor of the tank with only my head above the shimmering dark violet fluid that it contained. The mud cradled and caressed my tired body. Talmit loomed above me, holding what seemed to be a mass of entangled copper wires, but as he pressed the wires to my bare scalp they opened as of their own accord and their tips sought my skull and burrowed down through skin and bone into the hidden wrinkled grayness. I felt nothing more than tiny prickling sensations. 'The electrodes,' Talmit explained, 'seek out the centers of aging within your brain; we transmit signals that will induce a reversal of the normal processes of decay, and your brain will lose its perception of the direction of the flow of time. Your body thus will become more receptive to the stimulation it receives from the environment of the renewal tank. Close your eyes.'

Over my face he placed a breathing mask. He gave me a gentle shove, and the back of my head slipped from the edge of the tank, so that I floated out into the middle. The warmth increased. I dimly heard bubbling sounds. I imagined black sulfurous bubbles coming up from the mud and through the fluid in which I floated; I imagined that the fluid had turned the color of mud. Adrift in a tideless sea I lay, distantly aware that a current was passing over the electrodes, that something was tickling my brain, that I was engulfed in mud and in what could well have been an amniotic fluid. From far away came the deep voice of the Renewer Talmit summoning me to youth, drawing me back across the decades, unreeling time for me. There was a taste of salt in my mouth. Again I was crossing Earth Ocean, beset by pirates, defending my Watching equipment against their jeers and thrusts. Again I stood beneath the hot Aguptan sun meeting Avluela for the first time. I lived once more on Palash. I returned to the place of my birth in the western isles of the Lost Continents, in what formerly had been Usaamrik. I watched Roum fall a second time. Fragments of memories swam through my softening brain. There was no sequence, no rational unrolling of events. I was a child. I was a weary ancient. I was among the Rememberers. I visited the Somnambulists. I saw the Prince of Roum attempt to purchase eyes from an Artificer in Dijon. I bargained with the Procurator of Perris. I gripped the handles of my instruments and entered Watchfulness. I ate sweet things from a far-off world; I drew into my nostrils the perfume of springtime on Palash; I shivered in an old man's private winter; I swam in a surging sea, buoyant and happy; I sang; I wept; I resisted temptation; I yielded to temptations; I quarreled with Olmayne; I embraced Avluela; I experienced a flickering succession of nights and days as my biological clock moved in strange rhythms of reversal and acceleration. Illusions beset me. It rained fire from the sky; time rushed in several directions; I grew small and then enormous. I heard voices speaking in shades of scarlet and turquoise. Jagged music sparkled on the mountains. The sound of my drumming heartbeats was rough and fiery. I was trapped between strokes of my brain-piston, arms pressed to my sides so that I would occupy as little space as possible as it rammed itself home again and again and again. The stars throbbed, contracted, melted. Avluela said gently, 'We earn a second youthtime through the indulgent, benevolent impulses of the Will and through the performance of individual good works.' Olmayne said, 'How sleek I get!' Talmit said, 'These oscillations of perception signify only the dissolution of the wish toward self-destruction that lies at the heart of the aging process.' Gormon said, 'These perceptions of oscillation signify only the self-destruction of the wish toward dissolution that lies at the aging process of the heart.' The Procurator Manrule Seven said, 'We have been sent to this world as the devices of your purgation. We are instruments of the Will.' Earthclaim Nineteen said, 'On the other hand, permit me to disagree. The intersection of Earth's destinies and ours is purely accidental.' My eyelids turned to stone. The small creatures comprising my lungs began to flower. My skin sloughed off, revealing strands of muscle clinging to bone. Olmayne said, 'My pores grow smaller. My flesh grows tight. My breasts grow small.' Avluela said, 'Afterwards you will fly with us, Tomis.' The Prince of Roum covered his eyes with his hands. The towers of Roum swayed in the winds of the sun. I snatched a shawl from a passing Rememberer. Clowns wept in the streets of Perris. Talmit said, 'Awaken, now, Tomis, come up from it, open your eyes.'

'I am young again,' I said.

'Your renewal has only begun,' he said.

I could no longer move. Attendants seized me and swathed me in porous wrappings, and placed me on a rolling car, and took me to a second tank, much larger, in which dozens of people floated, each in a dreamy seclusion from the others. Their naked skulls were festooned with electrodes; their eyes were covered with pink tape; their hands were peacefully joined on their chests. Into this tank I went, and there were no illusions here, only a long slumber unbroken by dreams. This time I awakened to the sounds of a rushing tide, and found myself passing feet first through a constricted conduit into a sealed tank, where I breathed only fluid, and where I remained something more than a minute and something less than a century, while layers of skin were peeling from my soul. It was slow, taxing work. The Surgeons worked at a distance, their hands thrust into gloves that controlled the tiny flaying-knives, and they flensed me of evil with flick after flick after flick of the little blades, cutting

178

out guilt and sorrow, jealousy and rage, greed, lust, and impatience.

When they were done with me they opened the lid of the tank and lifted me out. I was unable to stand unaided. They attached instruments to my limbs that kneaded and massaged my muscles, restoring the tone. I walked again. I looked down at my bare body, strong and taut-fleshed and vigorous. Talmit came to me and threw a handful of mirror-dust into the air so that I could see myself; and as the tiny particles cohered, I peered at my gleaming reflection.

'No,' I said. 'You have the face wrong. I didn't look like that. The nose was sharper – the lips weren't so full – the hair not such a deep black—'

'We have worked from the records of the guild of Watchers, Tomis. You are more exactly a replica of your early self than your own memory realizes.'

'Can that be?'

'If you prefer, we can shape you to fit your self-conceptions and not reality. But it would be a frivolous thing to do, and it would take much time.'

'No,' I said. 'It hardly matters.'

He agreed. He informed me that I would have to remain in the house of renewal a while longer, until I was fully adapted to my new self. I was given the neutral clothes of a guildless one to wear, for I was without affiliation now; my status as Pilgrim had ended with my renewal, and I might now opt for any guild that would admit me once I left the house. 'How long did my renewal last?' I asked Talmit as I dressed. He replied, 'You came here in summer. Now it is winter. We do not work swiftly.'

'And how fares my companion Olmayne?'

'We failed with her.'

'I don't understand.'

'Would you like to see her?' Talmit asked.

'Yes,' I said, thinking that he would bring me to Olmayne's tank. I stood on a ramp looking down into a sealed container; Talmit indicated a fiber telescope, and I peered into its staring eye and beheld Olmayne. Or rather, what I was asked to believe was Olmayne. A naked girl-child of about eleven, smooth-skinned and breastless, lay curled up in the tank, knees drawn close to the flat chest, thumb thrust in mouth. At first I did not understand. Then the

179

child stirred, and I recognized the embryonic features of the regal Olmayne I had known: the wide mouth, the strong chin, the sharp, strong cheekbones. A dull shock of horror rippled through me, and I said to Talmit, 'What is this?'

'When the soul is too badly stained, Tomis, we must dig deep to cleanse it. Your Olmayne was a difficult case. We should not have attempted her; but she was insistent, and there were some indications that we might succeed with her. Those indications were in error, as you can see.'

'But what happened to her?'

'The renewal entered the irreversible stage before we could achieve a purging of her poisons,' Talmit said.

'You went too far? You made her too young?'

'As you can see. Yes.'

'What will you do? Why don't you get her out of there and let her grow up again?'

'You should listen more carefully, Tomis. I said the renewal is irreversible.'

'*Irreversible?*'

'She is lost in childhood's dreams. Each day she grows years younger. The inner clock whirls uncontrollably. Her body shrinks; her brain grows smooth. She enters babyhood shortly. She will never awaken.'

'And at the end—' I looked away. 'What then? A sperm and an egg, separating in the tank?'

'The retrogression will not go that far. She will die in infancy. Many are lost this way.'

'She spoke of the risks of renewal,' I said.

'Yet she insisted on our taking her. Her soul was dark, Tomis. She lived only for herself. She came to Jorslem to be cleansed, and now she has been cleansed, and she is at peace with the Will. Did you love her?'

'Never. Not for an instant.'

'Then what have you lost?'

'A segment of my past, perhaps.' I put my eye to the telescope again and beheld Olmayne, innocent now, restored to virginity, sexless, cleansed. At peace with the Will. I searched her oddly altered yet familiar face for an insight into her dreams. Had she known what was befalling her, as she tumbled helplessly into youthfulness? Had she cried out in anguish and frustration when she felt her life slipping away? Had there been a final flare of the old imperious Olmayne,

180

before she sank into this unwanted purity? The child in the tank was smiling. The supple little body uncoiled, then drew more tightly into a huddled ball. Olmayne was at peace with the Will. Suddenly, as though Talmit had spread another mirror in the air, I looked into my own new self, and saw what had been done for me, and knew that I had been granted another life with the proviso that I make something more of it than I had of my first one, and I felt humbled, and pledged myself to serve the Will, and I was engulfed in joy that came in mighty waves, like the surging tides of Earth Ocean, and I said farewell to Olmayne, and asked Talmit to take me to another place.

11

AND Avluela came to me in my room in the house of renewal, and we both were frightened when we met. The jacket she wore left her bunched-up wings bare; they seemed hardly under her control at all, but fluttered nervously, starting to open a short way, their gossamer tips expanding in little quivering flickers. Her eyes were large and solemn; her face looked more lean and pointed than ever. We stared in silence at one another a long while; my skin grew warm, my vision hazy; I felt the churning of inner forces that had not pulled at me in decades, and I feared them even as I welcomed them.

'Tomis?' she said finally, and I nodded.

She touched my shoulders, my arms, my lips. And I put my fingers to her wrists, her flanks, and then, hesitantly, to the shallow bowls of her breasts. Like two who had lost their sight we learned each other by touch. We were strangers. That withered old Watcher she had known and perhaps loved had gone, banished for the next fifty years or more, and in his place stood someone mysteriously transformed, unknown, unmet. The old Watcher had been a sort of father to her; what was this guildless young Tomis supposed to be? And what was she to me, a daughter no longer? I did not know myself of myself. I was alien to my sleek, taut skin. I was perplexed and delighted by the juices that now flowed, by the throbbings and swellings that I had nearly forgotten.

'Your eyes are the same,' she said. 'I would always know you by your eyes.'

'What have you done these many months, Avluela?'

'I have been flying every night. I flew to Agupt and deep into Afreek. Then I returned and flew to Stanbool. When it gets dark, I go aloft. Do you know, Tomis, I feel truly alive only when I'm up there?'

'You are of the Fliers. It is in the nature of your guild to feel that way.'

'One day we'll fly side by side, Tomis.'

I laughed at that. 'The old Surgeries are closed, Avluela. They work wonders here, but they can't transform me into a Flier. One must be born with wings.'

'One doesn't need wings to fly.'

'I know. The invaders lift themselves without the help of wings. I saw you, one day soon after Roum fell – you and Gormon in the sky together—' I shook my head. 'But I am no invader either.'

'You will fly with me, Tomis. We'll go aloft, and not only by night, even though my wings are merely nightwings. In bright sunlight we'll soar together.'

Her fantasy pleased me. I gathered her into my arms, and she was cool and fragile against me, and my own body pulsed with new heat. For a while we talked no more of flying, though I drew back from taking what she offered at that moment, and was content merely to caress her. One does not awaken in a single lunge.

Later we walked through the corridors, passing others who were newly renewed, and we went into the great central room whose ceiling admitted the winter sunlight, and studied each other by that changing pale light, and walked, and talked again. I leaned a bit on her arm, for I did not have all my strength yet, and so in a sense it was as it had been for us in the past, the girl helping the old dodderer along. When she saw me back to my room, I said, 'Before I was renewed, you told me of a new guild of Redeemers. I—'

'There is time for that later,' she said, displeased.

In my room we embraced, and abruptly I felt the full fire of the renewed leap up within me, so that I feared I might consume her cool slim body. But it is a fire that does not consume – it only kindles its counterpart in others. In her ecstasy her wings unfolded until I was wrapped in their silken softness. And as I gave myself to the violence of joy, I knew I would not need again to lean on her arm.

We ceased to be strangers; we ceased to feel fear with one another. She came to me each day at my exercise time, and I walked with her, matching her stride for stride. And the fire burned even higher and more brightly for us.

Talmit was with me frequently too. He showed me the arts of using my renewed body, and helped me successfully grow youthful. I declined his invitation to view Olmayne once more. One day he told me that her retrogression had

183

come to its end. I felt no sorrow over that, just a curious brief emptiness that soon passed.

'You will leave here soon,' the Renewer said. 'Are you ready?'

'I think so.'

'Have you given much thought to your destination after this house?'

'I must seek a new guild, I know.'

'Many guilds would have you, Tomis. But which do you want?'

'The guild in which I would be most useful to mankind,' I said. 'I owe the Will a life.'

Talmit said, 'Has the Flier girl spoken to you of the possibilities before you?'

'She mentioned a newly founded guild.'

'Did she give it a name?'

'The guild of Redeemers.'

'What do you know of it?'

'Very little,' I said.

'Do you wish to know more?'

'If there is more to know.'

'I am of the guild of Redeemers,' Talmit said. 'So is the Flier Avluela.'

'You both are already guilded! How can you belong to more than one guild? Only the Dominators were permitted such freedom; and they—'

'Tomis, the guild of Redeemers accepts members from all other guilds. It is the supreme guild, as the guild of Dominators once was. In its ranks are Rememberers and Scribes, Indexers, Servitors, Fliers, Landholders, Somnambulists, Surgeons, Clowns, Merchants, Vendors. There are Changelings as well, and—'

'Changelings?' I gasped. 'They are outside all guilds, by law! How can a guild embrace Changelings?'

'This is the guild of Redeemers. Even Changelings may win redemption, Tomis.'

Chastened, I said, 'Even Changelings, yes. But how strange it is to think of such a guild!'

'Would you despise a guild that embraces Changelings?'

'I find this guild difficult to comprehend.'

'Understanding will come at the proper time.'

'When is the proper time?'

184

'The day you leave this place,' said Talmit.

That day arrived shortly. Avluela came to fetch me. I stepped forth uncertainly into Jorslem's springtime to complete the ritual of renewal. Talmit had instructed her on how to guide me. She took me through the city to the holy places, so that I could worship at each of the shrines. I knelt at the wall of the Hebers and at the gilded dome of the Mislams; then I went down into the lower part of the city, through the marketplace, to the gray, dark, ill-fashioned building covering the place where the god of the Christers is said to have died; then I went to the spring of knowledge and the fountain of the Will, and from there to the guild-house of the guild of Pilgrims to surrender my mask and robes and starstone, and thence to the wall of the Old City. At each of these places I offered myself to the Will with words I had waited long to speak. Pilgrims and ordinary citizens of Jorslem gathered at a respectful distance; they knew that I had been lately renewed and hoped that some emanation from my new youthful body would bring them good fortune. At last my obligations were fulfilled. I was a free man in full health, able now to choose the quality of the life I wished to lead.

Avluela said, 'Will you come with me to the Redeemers now?'

'Where will we find them? In Jorslem?'

'In Jorslem, yes. A meeting will convene in an hour's time for the purpose of welcoming you into membership.'

From her tunic she drew something small and gleaming, which I recognized in bewilderment as a starstone. 'What are you doing with that?' I asked. 'Only Pilgrims—'

'Put your hand over mine,' she said, extending a fist in which the starstone was clenched.

I obeyed. Her small pinched face grew rigid with concentration for a moment. Then she relaxed. She put the starstone away.

'Avluela, what—?'

'A signal to the guild,' she said gently. 'A notice to them to gather now that you are on your way.'

'How did you get that stone?'

'Come with me,' she said. 'Oh, Tomis, if only we could fly there! But it is not far. We meet almost in the shadow of the house of renewal. Come, Tomis. Come!'

185

12

THERE was no light in the room. Avluela led me into the subterranean blackness, and told me that I had reached the guildhall of the Redeemers, and left me standing by myself. 'Don't move,' she cautioned.

I sensed the presence of others in the room about me. But I heard nothing and saw nothing.

Something was thrust toward me.

Avluela said, 'Put out your hands. What do you feel?'

I touched a small square cabinet resting, perhaps, on a metal framework. Along its face were familiar dials and levers. My groping hands found handles rising from the cabinet's upper surface. At once it was as though all my renewal had been undone, and the conquest of Earth canceled as well: I was a Watcher again, for surely this was a Watcher's equipment!

I said, 'It is not the same cabinet I once had. But it is not greatly different.'

'Have you forgotten your skills, Tomis?'

'I think they remain with me even now.'

'Use the machine, then,' said Avluela. 'Do your Watching once more, and tell me what you see.'

Easily and happily I slipped into the old attitudes. I performed the preliminary rituals quickly, clearing my mind of doubts and frictions. It was surprisingly simple to bring myself into a spirit of Watchfulness; I had not attempted it since the night Earth fell, and yet it seemed to me that I was able to enter the state more rapidly than in the old days.

Now I grasped the handles. How strange they were! They did not terminate in the grips to which I was accustomed: rather, something cool and hard was mounted at the tip of each handle. A gem of some kind, perhaps. Possibly even a starstone, I realized. My hands closed over the twin coolnesses. I felt a moment of apprehension, even of raw fear.

Then I regained the necessary tranquillity, and my soul flooded into the device before me, and I began to Watch.

In my Watchfulness I did not soar to the stars, as I had in the old days. Although I perceived, my perception was limited to the immediate surroundings of my room. Eyes closed, body hunched in trance, I reached out and came first to Avluela; she was near me, almost upon me. I saw her plainly. She smiled; she nodded; her eyes were aglow.

— I love you.

— Yes, Tomis. And we will be together always.

— I have never felt so close to another person.

— In this guild we are all close, all the time. We are the Redeemers, Tomis. We are new. Nothing like this has been on Earth before.

— How am I speaking to you, Avluela?

— Your mind speaks to mine through the machine. And some day the machine will not be needed.

— And then we will fly together?

— Long before then, Tomis.

The starstones grew warm in my hands. I clearly perceived the instrument, now: a Watcher's cabinet, but with certain modifications, among them the starstones mounted on the handles. And I looked beyond Avluela and saw other faces, ones that I knew. The austere figure of the Renewer Talmit was to my left. Beside him stood the Surgeon with whom I had journey to Jorslem, with the Changeling Bernalt at his elbow, and now at last I knew what business it was that had brought these men of Nayrub to the holy city. The others I did not recognize; but there were two Fliers, and a Rememberer grasping his shawl, and a woman Servitor, and others. And I saw them all by an inner light for the room was as dark as it had been when I entered it. Not only did I see them, but I touched them, mind to mind.

The mind I touched first was Bernalt's. I met it easily though fearfully, drew back, met it again. He greeted me and welcomed me. I realized then that only if I could look upon a Changeling as my brother could I, and Earth itself, win the sought-for redemption. For until we were truly one people, how could we earn an end to our punishment?

I tried to enter Bernalt's mind but I was afraid. How

187

could I hide those prejudices, those petty contempts, those conditioned reflexes with which we unavoidably think of Changelings?

'Hide nothing,' he counseled. 'Those things are no secret to me. Give them up now and join me.'

I struggled. I cast out demons. I summoned up the memory of the moment outside the Changeling shrine, after Bernalt had saved us, when I had invited him to journey with us. How had I felt then toward him? Had I regarded him, at least for a moment, as a brother?

I amplified that moment of gratitude and companionship. I let it swell, and blaze, and it obliterated the encrustations of scorn and empty distain; and I saw the human soul beneath the strange Changeling surface, and I broke through that surface and found the path to redemption. He drew me toward his mind.

I joined Bernalt, and he enrolled me in his guild. I was of the Redeemers now.

Through my mind rolled a voice, and I did not know whether I heard the resonant boom of Talmit, or the dry ironic tone of the Surgeon, or Bernalt's controlled murmur, or Avluela's soft whisper, for it was all these voices at once, and others, and they said:

'When all mankind is enrolled in our guild, we will be conquered no longer. When each of us is part of every other one of us, our sufferings will end. There is no need for us to struggle against our conquerors, for we will absorb them, once we are all Redeemed. Enter us, Tomis who was the Watcher Wuellig.'

And I entered.

And I became the Surgeon and the Flier and the Renewer and the Changeling and the Servitor and the rest. And they became me. And so long as my hands gripped the starstones we were of one soul and one mind. This was not the merging of communion, in which a Pilgrim sinks anonymously into the Will, but rather a union of self and self, maintaining independence within a larger dependence. It was the keen perception one gets from Watching coupled with the submergence in a larger entity that one gets from communion, and I knew this was something wholly new on

Earth, not merely the founding of a new guild but the initiation of a new cycle of human existence, the birth of the Fourth Cycle upon this defeated planet.

The voice said, 'Tomis, we will Redeem those in greatest need first. We will go into Agupt, into the desert where miserable Changelings huddle in an ancient building that they worship, and we will take them into us and make them clean again. We will go on, to the west, to a pitful village smitten by the crystallization disease, and we will reach the souls of the villagers and free them from taint, and the crystallization will cease and their bodies will be healed. And we will go on beyond Agupt, to all the lands of the world, and find those who are without guilds, and those who are without hope, and those who are without tomorrows, and we will give them life and purpose again. And a time will come when all Earth is Redeemed.'

They put a vision before me of a transformed planet, and of the harsh-faced invaders yielding peacefully to us and begging to be incorporated into that new thing that had germinated in the midst of their conquest. They showed me an Earth that had been purged of its ancient sins.

Then I felt it was time to withdraw my hands from the machine I grasped, and I withdrew my hands.

The vision ebbed. The glow faded. But yet I was no longer alone in my skull, for some contact lingered, and the room ceased to be dark.

'How did this happen?' I asked. 'When did this begin?'

'In the days after the conquest,' said Talmit, 'we asked ourselves why we had fallen so easily, and how we could lift ourselves above what we had been. We saw that our guilds had not provided enough of a structure for our lives, that some closer union was our way to redemption. We had the starstones; we had the instruments of Watching; all that remained was to fuse them.'

The Surgeon said, 'You will be important to us, Tomis, because you understand how to throw your mind forth. We seek former Watchers. They are the nucleus of our guild. Once your soul roved the stars to search out mankind's enemies; now it will roam the Earth to bring mankind together.'

189

Avluela said, 'You will help me to fly, Tomis, even by day. And you will fly beside me.'

'When do you leave?' I asked.

'Now,' she said. 'I go to Agupt, to the temple of the Changelings, to offer them what we have to offer. And all of us will join to give me strength, and that strength will be focused through you, Tomis.' Her hands touched mine. Her lips brushed mine. 'The life of Earth begins again, now, this year, this new cycle. Oh, Tomis, we are all reborn!'

13

I remained alone in the room. The others scattered.
Avluela went above, into the street. I put my hands to the
mounted starstones, and I saw her as clearly as though she
stood beside me. She was preparing herself for flight. First
she put off her clothing, and her bare body glistened in the
afternoon sun. Her little body seemed impossibly delicate;
a strong wind would shatter her, I thought. Then she knelt,
bowed, made her ritual. She spoke to herself, yet I heard
her words, the words Fliers say as they ready themselves to
leave the ground. All guilds are one in this new guild; we
have no secrets from one another; there are no mysteries.
And as she beseeched the favor of the Will and the support
of all her kind, my prayers joined with hers.

She rose and let her wings unfold. Some passers-by
looked oddly at her, not because there was anything unusual
about the sight of a naked Flier in the streets of Jorslem,
but because the sunlight was so strong and her transparent
wings, so lightly stained with pigment, were evidently
nightwings, incapable of withstanding the pressure of the
solar wind.

'I love you,' we said to her, and our hands ran lightly
over her satiny skin in a brief caress.

Her nostrils flickered in delight. Her small girl-child's
breasts became agitated. Her wings now were fully spread,
and they gleamed wonderously in the sunlight.

'Now we fly to Agupt,' she murmured, 'to Redeem the
Changelings and make them one with us, Tomis, will you
come with me?'

'I will be with you,' we said, and I gripped the starstones tightly and crouched over my cabinet of instruments
in the dark room beneath the place where she stood. 'We
will fly together, Avluela.'

'Up then,' she said, and we said, 'Up.'

Her wings beat, curving to take the wind, and we felt
her struggling in the first moment, and we gave her the

strength she needed, and she took it as it poured from us through me to her, and we rose high. The spires and parapets of Jorslem the golden grew small, and the city became a pink dot in the green hills, and Avluela's throbbing wings thrust her swiftly westward, toward the setting sun, toward the land of Agupt. Her ecstasy swept through us all. 'See, Tomis, how wonderful it is, far above everything? Do you feel it?'

'I feel it,' I whispered. 'The cool wind against bare flesh – the wind in my hair – we drift on the currents, we coast, we soar, Avluela, we soar!'

To Agupt. To the sunset.

We looked down at sparkling Lake Medit. In the distance somewhere was Land Bridge. To the north, Eyrop. To the south, Afreek. Far ahead, beyond Earth Ocean, lay my homeland. Later I would return there, flying westward with Avluela, bringing the good news of Earth's transformation.

From this height one could not tell that our world had ever been conquered. One saw only the beauty of the colors of the land and the sea, not the checkpoints of the invaders.

Those checkpoints would not long endure. We would conquer our conquerors, not with weapons but with love; and as the Redemption of Earth became universal we would welcome into our new self even the beings who had seized our planet.

'I knew that some day you would fly beside me, Tomis,' said Avluela.

In my dark room I sent new surges of power through her wings.

She hovered over the desert. The old Surgery, the Changeling shrine, would soon be in sight. I grieved that we would have to come down. I wished we could stay aloft forever, Avluela and I.

'We will, Tomis, we will!' she told me. 'Nothing can separate us now! You believe that, don't you, Tomis?'

'Yes,' we said, 'I believe that.' And we guided her down through the darkening sky.